HE SAID SHE SAID

tristan & emma

Shannon Layne

EPIC
Press

Tristan & Emma
He Said She Said: Book #6

Written by Shannon Layne

Copyright © 2016 by Abdo Consulting Group, Inc.

Published by EPIC Press™
PO Box 398166
Minneapolis, MN 55439

Printed in the United States of America.

Cover design and illustration by Candice Keimig
Edited by Marianna Baer

LIBRARY OF CONGRESS CATALOGING-IN-PUBLICATION DATA

Layne, Shannon.
Tristan & Emma / Shannon Layne.
p. cm. — (He said, she said)
Summary: Emma has a heart turned against love until she comes to New England
for the summer and meets Tristan. When he sees Emma for the first time, he is
enchanted with her, forcing himself to ask the question; can a heart can be turned
toward love before it's too late.
ISBN 978-1-68076-041-5 (hardcover)
1. Summer romance—Fiction. 2. Interpersonal relations—Fiction. 3. High school
students—Fiction. 4. Young adult fiction. I. Title.
[Fic]—dc23
2015932729

EPICPRESS.COM

For my Emily, the one who taught me that true love doesn't just exist in fairy tales

emma

Whenever I used to think of home, the same picture came into my head like paint splashing onto a canvas. I could see a sky so blue it hurt my eyes, the red-and-white-checkered pattern of the blanket we used for picnics. I'd smell salty air, and I'd feel the bite of the wind on my cheeks. I could hear my mother on the piano, the lilting notes of Beethoven, and smell cookies baking in the oven. It was a simple image, but it was home.

Now, when I think of home, all I see is his face. The notes of the piano fade into the sound of his voice, the warmth from his chest where he holds me in his arms.

Home used to be a simple image, a place where I was comfortable and happy. Now, nothing is simple. Now, nowhere is home unless he is there with me.

tristan

I remember, one day that summer, when we were sitting on the very edge of the pier while a storm rolled in. Emma had her feet bare, dangling in the water. Her fingers were tangled in mine and her eyes were focused on my face as if she was looking at something amazing. I don't even remember what I was talking about. It was some random story about me as a kid, or something like that. But she sat quietly, and she held my hand and brushed my hair out of my face. She gazed at me the entire time like all she cared about in the world was sitting next to me on those creaky boards.

Never in my life will I forget the way she looked at me that day.

CHAPTER 1

emma

My dad says I was born at the exact moment the storm ended. It had been nothing but thunder and lightning for three days, he said, and then just as I entered the world, everything went quiet.

"It was a miracle," he would say as he told the story. "Your mom had been in labor for nearly twelve hours. The rain hadn't stopped once. Then, right as you were born, the whole world stopped to pay attention."

I used to live with him and my mom. That was a long time ago; they've been divorced since I was in junior high. They started fighting when I was little, trying to work things out for years before they finally called it off. The custody battle was ferocious, but relatively brief; the details are hard to remember. When my parents got divorced, my dad's lawyers convinced the judge that my mom's drinking problem (which I had never seen) was a danger to me. Most custody cases favor the mom's side. Not this time; my dad was awarded almost full custody.

It's been a long time since all of that happened. My dad moved to Massachusetts when I was a sophomore in high school and when I told my mom I wanted to go, she didn't fight it, even though the extra distance meant she'd see me even less often. I guess I just wanted to try and start over. My new life hadn't been easy to adjust to. I saw the pain in her face but she was never one to make me do something I didn't want to do.

Now I'm headed back to the east coast to visit her. After I graduated from high school, a couple of my friends and I headed to San Diego and got an apartment together. Both of them are going to school part-time. I wasn't sure about college so I got a job as a waitress and have been doing that ever since.

I glance out the airplane window and trace my fingertips along the edge, as though if I wish hard enough I can escape through the barrier.

Even though I love my mom, I don't think I've ever felt so torn about coming to visit. My room-mates will be going abroad, or living the beach life, and I'm headed to the town in Rhode Island where I grew up until my parents divorced to help my mom open her bed and breakfast. She's been working on it for almost as long as I can remember. I have old friends there who have known me since I was little, but I haven't been back in so long that I've lost touch with most of them. I can't say I'm exactly excited to spend my summer in a place where I don't know anyone, and work with my mom, and yet, I'm still going. I guess staying in San Diego and working all summer doesn't exactly appeal to me, either. When I first moved and started working it seemed like a great idea, but lately it's been a struggle just to get myself up and out the door. I run my hands through my hair and sigh. I think I need a change. I just wish I knew what that change was supposed to be.

A voice over the airplane speaker knocks me out of my thoughts to announce that we'll be landing in Boston in twenty minutes. I adjust my seat back to its upright position and shove my backpack under the seat in front of me. The descent makes my stomach turn. I yank out my headphones and close my eyes, gripping my seat handles so tightly I start to lose the feeling in my fingers, and wait to land.

CHAPTER 2
emma

My mom stands out in the crowd of people waiting at the gate like a rose in a garden of daisies. She has dark red hair that she always wears pulled back, and she's tall and willowy. She plays the piano, studied at Julliard. Her fingers are long, her hands graceful. I spot her in the crowd almost as soon as I step off the plane, and I tuck a strand of my hair that's come loose behind my ear the way it always does. She sees me, and her face lights up, a big smile brightening her features. Even with my mixed feelings about being here, seeing her makes me so happy. I can't help but smile back, hurrying toward her, until finally I drop my bags and I'm in her arms. Her arms around me transport me back to a time when things were simpler, when I was a child and secure in the knowledge that I was loved, that just being near her meant everything was okay.

"Oh, my Emma," she murmurs, laying her cheek against my hair. "It's been so long."

She smells like she always does, lemon verbena and roses. I feel the familiar stab of guilt for spending so much time away from her, especially since I've been in California, and wrap my arms tighter around her waist. Finally, she releases me and leans down to help me with my bags.

"Your hair is so long," she comments as we head to the door. "And so blonde from the sun."

My hair has undertones of red, a gift from my mom, but it's much lighter than hers.

"I haven't cut it in a while," I say. My hair is so thick and heavy that I usually don't let it grow so long because it becomes a pain. It's hanging in waves nearly to my waist as it is.

In the car on the way home, my mom fiddles with the pearl necklace she never takes off, the only sign that she's nervous.

"I can't wait for you to see it," she says. "I've done so much work since I saw you last. The shutters have been painted, the upstairs veranda is completely new . . ."

She's talking about the house that passed down from her grandmother; it's been in her family forever, but had been empty for years when my mom started working on it. It was her project after the divorce, after my dad and I left. She emptied the trust fund her parents left for her and poured it all into the house. It's taken her years to fix it up. The estate itself was in bad shape. The entire place needed new floors and a new roof and an updated plumbing system, and it's a big property: three stories, six bedrooms and bathrooms.

I have memories of visiting it when I was little, pretending it was a castle that once belonged to a long-gone princess. I would walk through it step by careful step, avoiding rotting floorboards and cobwebs. There were parts of the house in such bad shape that my mom wouldn't let me go near them at all, like the kitchen and most of the lower deck. The stairs were okay though, and I would take them all the way to the top floor. There was a room on the east side of the house at the tallest point, the tower room. The door was almost hidden in the corner of the hallway, but I sought it out every time just so I could go into the tower. The floors were still solid enough to hold my weight, and the brick walls were barely crumbled. Everything may have been coated in a layer of dust and there were places that ivy was starting to invade, but I didn't care. To me it was a haven, a place where spells had been broken and love had been found. A slanted window looked out onto the Atlantic Ocean, and I would lean out and let the wind tease my hair. I would stay there until my mother called me back down. I haven't thought about the tower in a long time.

"Do you remember when you were little and we would visit the house?" my mom is saying. "You used to go straight to the tower room and pretend you were a princess. You would stay up there for hours while I puttered around the house, wondering when I'd ever be able to fix it up."

I nod, still facing the window.

It's strange that my mom was thinking of the exact same memory that just crossed my mind. And it stings a little to hear her mention it. Some of my favorite memories of childhood are of playing in that tower, or singing with my mom at the piano, my dad singing off-key in the background. But I also remember when all the music stopped. I remember when everything I imagined when I was in the tower faded away like a dream does when you wake up, until it's just a distant memory. I know knights in shining armor don't really exist, and I know that no matter how much time I spend looking to the horizon, no one is going to come and rescue me.

"It's been a long time since I believed in fairy tales," I say just as my mom stops the car at the end of the long graveled drive. I open the door and shade my eyes at the house.

My jaw drops.

"Mom . . . " I trail off as the words get lost between my head and my throat. The last time I saw the house, half the roof still needed shingles and all the windows were missing their shutters. The paint was chipped and cracking, and the boards of the wrap-around porch were rotting away. The house I am looking at bears no resemblance to that run-down place at all. It sparkles in the afternoon light, with fresh white paint coating all three stories and new blue shutters on every window. The balconies on the second and third story have delicate railings and there are summer roses climbing every single trellis. The manicured yard surrounds the house, with sugar maples and hickory, creating a shady canopy. But the house is center stage, stealing my attention. A wooden sign hangs at the edge of the driveway in swirled blue letters. The gravel road skirts around the side of the house and leads right down to the beach. I can hear the waves caressing the sand, and the breeze from the ocean cools my sun-warmed face.

"Mom, it's amazing. It's . . . " I wave my hands in the air, at a total loss. "It's perfect."

My mom smiles. "Did you see the sign?" she asks.

"Yeah, I saw. It's really pretty."

"Read it."

I look over at the sign again, reading the scripted words more carefully. My eyes fill with tears.

EMMA'S CASTLE BY THE SEA

"Mom, you didn't have to do this," I whisper.

Her hand slips into mine, and I stare at the house she built for me.

CHAPTER 3

emma

The oak double doors of the inn open into a parlor that looks completely different from when I last saw it. Leather couches and cozy armchairs draped with colorful blankets are nestled in front of a brick and stone fireplace. The floors are so shiny I can see my reflection in them and the dark wood adds a touch of sophistication. My mom is watching me, judging my reaction. I think she's waiting for me to say something, but I'm completely speechless. I've never seen anything so beautiful, a place that looks elegant and so homey at the same time. A huge spiraling staircase leads upstairs to more bedrooms, including mine and my mom's, which are situated in a private wing on the west side of the house.

I climb the staircase and enter my room, dropping my bags at the door. There's a plush, new cushion on the big bay window that overlooks Narragansett Bay, while a cheerful yellow rug warms the dark hardwood floors. The antique bedframe has been mine since I was little, the iron headboard's swirling curlicues painted white by my mom. A white goose-down comforter lies softly over the bed, with the quilt my grandma made for me folded across the foot. A white door opens into my own bathroom, which has the big claw foot tub that I remember but with a new showerhead installed and a shower curtain hanging from a rail. New, fluffy towels hang on the drying rack, and everywhere there are little touches from my mom. Tiny Mason jars filled with sand and seashells sit on the dresser, and on the wall above the bed's headboard is a panoramic photo of a sunset. I recognize it instantly—I took it and gave it to my mom for Mother's Day a few years ago. Every year

I create something special just for her. It's been my tradition since the divorce.

I stand and stare, open-mouthed. "I can't believe you did all this," I whisper. "It's beautiful."

My mom gives me a shy smile and fusses with the sweater tied around her shoulders. For the first time, I notice how thin she's become.

"I wanted it to be perfect," she says. "It was a rush to finish it all before you arrived, but somehow it all came together. The dresser is new. The bed is the same, obviously. I'll never get rid of it."

I step over to the dresser, which has been painted a distressed white. My mom likes to pick up furniture from flea markets and antique stores and fix them up and I see quickly that this is one of her projects. I'm overwhelmed by the amount of effort my mom has put into this place. Her personal touch is everywhere. Regret surges through me that I wasn't a bigger part of it. I've been in and out of this place throughout the duration of the renovations, but I could never imagine the finished product the way my mom could.

"I moved the piano into the library downstairs," my mom says. The muscles in my back stiffen. I grew up in a house full of music—my mother on the piano is one of my earliest memories. One night, when I was little, I walked into my parents' bedroom to ask her to play for me and found them screaming at each other. Both were totally oblivious to my presence as I stood there in my cotton nightgown, frightened into immobility until my mom turned and saw me crying in the corner. As she scooped me up, I felt her tears soak into the cotton on my shoulder. The sound of the piano was never the same for me after that night. I would hear her playing after a fight with my father, late at night after I'd gone to bed, and the melodies she coaxed from the keys tore me apart. I have trouble hearing it, even now.

"I'm going to start unpacking," is all I say.

My mom nods and smiles at me, but it doesn't quite reach her eyes.

"I have cookie dough downstairs," she says. "Molasses, your favorite. I'll go put some in the oven."

I listen to her footsteps fade stair by stair and turn back to my room. The picture above my bed mirrors the pinks and purples of the sky outside, and I have a sudden need to capture it. I grab my camera and take every other stair down to the first floor and head outside, circling around the back of the house to the floating dock that juts out into the cove. The beach is rocky and edged in tide pools that I know are filled with sea stars and anemones; the sea is quiet as I run down the little dock. I stop at the very edge. It rocks gently from my steps, and I reach my hands out toward the colored sky as though I could touch it if I wanted it enough. A song comes to my head, and for the first time in a long time I let the notes escape my lips.

"Come with me, tiptoe on the waves
My darling, my little one
Across the sea, through the blue we'll go
Til the midnight moon turns to sun . . . "

It's a lullaby my mom used to sing to me when I was little. The notes carry in the wind and over the water, and in the fading light of the sun I see a sailboat crossing the horizon. I almost let myself pre-tend it's a pirate ship sailing in from Neverland, then catch myself. Like I told my mom, I don't believe in fairy tales anymore.

CHAPTER 4
tristan

I'm guiding a sailboat into the harbor when I see her, standing on the edge of the dock in the fading light. Her hair is like a candle flame, waving in the wind, and her silhouette shimmers on the water. I swear I catch the melody of a song, carried by the wind, but then it disappears and I know it must have been my imagination. I turn my attention back to the boat, guiding it toward our slip inside the harbor, and when I glance back she's gone. I'm not sure if she was real, or a trick of the dimming light.

I guide the boat in and tie up, then thank my two customers. When I'm finished, I turn and squint toward where I thought I saw the girl, but it's too dark now to tell. I can barely see the dock where she was standing. I fold my arms across my chest, frowning. She reminded me of something so familiar, but I can't quite put my finger on it. And then it hits me, like a dream right before you wake up and it slips away.

There's a painting that hangs in the hallway of my parents' house that's probably been there since before I was born. It shows a mermaid sitting on rocks by the seashore, set against the wreckage of the ships she lured to their dooms with her beautiful voice. I remember asking my dad about it when I was young.

"The sea is a dangerous thing, son," my dad said, trying to answer my earnest six-year-old question. "That's true enough. But mermaids aren't real. That's only a painting." He tousled my hair as I nodded, but I wasn't sure he was right.

When I was growing up, more than once I could have sworn I heard one singing. I would stand on the dock or the deck of one of our boats and the sound would come from somewhere deep down in the water, a haunting melody that always disappeared just quickly enough to make me question whether I'd heard it at all. Even though I've spent probably half of my life on the sea, I've still never seen one.

My earliest memory is of water: whether it's Ethan, my older brother, throwing me into the harbor, or my father teaching me to tie ropes, to hoist a mainsail, to tie a bowline. My family owns a boat chartering business, and I've been a part of it since I was old enough to walk down a dock. Since I graduated from high school two years ago, I do everything from private sails for two to taking one of our yachts with twenty people for a cruise around the bay. I also help out with maintenance and repairs when my dad needs me. I'm good with my hands and familiar with the framework of each one of our vessels. More than that, I know every inch of this harbor, of this part of the ocean, although I'd rather spend my time sailing it myself than carrying tourists around.

I finish tying up the boat and head up the dock

toward the charterhouse. My dad should still be there finishing today's paperwork, and then we're supposed to head home together.

The charterhouse serves as the headquarters for Beyond the Sand, our boat chartering business. My mom came up with that one.

The glass door chimes as I open it, and our old black Labrador, Boone, comes up to lick my hands. He comes to work with my dad every single morning. Wherever he is, you can bet Boone is less than three feet away.

"Hey buddy," I murmur, stroking his ears. "Dad? Are you ready to go?"

My dad emerges from the side room with a mound of papers in his hands and his glasses slipping off his nose. I take the papers from his arms and set them on the desk before he can protest. He's got a bad back, and lately, it's been even worse. I've talked with him about letting me expand the business myself, but he's been stubborn about the direction I want to take the company. I just think we can do more than taxi people around the bay, but that's a conversation for another day.

"Hey, tadpole," he says, and I wince. He's been calling me that since I was two and I still can't hear it without turning red. "How was the run with the Thompsons?"

"It was weird," I answer, shuffling the pile of papers. My dad sits down and leans back in the worn desk chair with a sigh. "Mrs. Thompson didn't say a word the entire time. I think she's still mad at him."

"Well, you would be too if you found out that your husband was cheating on you with the florist. He put some effort into arranging this trip as a way to make it up to her, but I don't think a sailboat ride in the harbor is going to do it."

I snort. In our small community, scandals like theirs get around pretty fast.

"Did you see the bed and breakfast on your way back in? Looks like it'll be ready to open up soon. Your mom noticed it the other day."

"Yeah, actually. I saw it for a second."

"Looks pretty nice."

"Who owns it again?"

"That LaVallie woman. She's the one who's been working on it for so long."

I think about the figure on the dock but it doesn't fit the image I have of the tall, slender woman who has kept to herself, working on that place, for years. "Does she have a daughter?"

My dad gets up and starts switching off the lights, shutting down for the night. "Yeah, she has a daughter. But she's never here. Lives with her dad most of the time."

We head toward the truck, the humid night air wrapping us like a blanket.

"I think she's back."

My dad gives me a sideways glance. "Did you see her?" he asks as we open the doors.

"I thought I did. But it could have been a trick of the light."

My dad starts the truck and we start to drive away, heading east, toward home. The image fills my mind over and over again: the way the sunset played over the waves, and the silhouette of the girl against the sky. The entire drive home I hear the melody I thought I imagined in my head, over and over again, a siren call I can't get out of my mind.

CHAPTER 5

tristan

A few days later, I wake up to the unbelievably obnoxious sound of Ethan's voice.

"Get up, little brother," he says, tossing pillows at my head. "I have a business proposition for you."

I sit up, rubbing my eyes, and check the time. Ethan is never up earlier than me. My watch says six a.m.

"What the fuck?" I grumble. "What's going on?"

Ethan waltzes over to my bed, grabbing the chair from my desk on his way. "Sorry to wake you so early. I'm taking out a tour in an hour and I wanted to catch you before I left. We have a double date tonight."

"That's really romantic, Ethan, but you're not really my type."

Ethan smiles—a big shit-eating grin, the one that means he's up to something. I can't tell you how many times I saw that look on his face when we were kids. It always meant somebody was about to get in trouble. And usually, that somebody was me.

"It's with Jenny."

"Jenny Chancellor?"

"That's her."

My brother has had a crush on Jenny Chancellor for years. She's about two years older than me, the same age as Ethan. She was the same year as him in high school.

"What made her finally say yes?" I'm skeptical of this whole endeavor, but amused at the same time.

"I'm not sure. I saw her last night at Riley's with a bunch of her friends and she agreed to let us take her for a sail."

"Us? That's the weird part here, bud."

"I know, I know. But that's how I got her to

say yes. She wanted to bring along one of her girl-friends, so I told her we'd make it a double date."

"Which friend? I might be more interested once I hear who it is."

"I'm not sure. She only said her first name. Emma."

"That's all you know?"

"Yup. That and that she doesn't live here. She's visiting her mom for the summer. Come on, Tris. Jenny's cute. I bet her friend's hot, too."

"I'm not sure that's how it works," I say distractedly. I haven't had a date in a while. My last girlfriend hung around for six months or so until we burned out on each other. My work schedule makes it even harder, with the amount of tours I volunteer to take on top of the amount of time I already spend on the water. I weigh the cost of an evening to myself against the possibility that I might actually like this Emma girl. What the hell. I could use a little distraction.

"I'm in," I say impulsively. "What time?"

"They're meeting us on the dock at eight," says Ethan.

"Sounds good to me."

I live in an addition right behind my parents' house that I helped build when I graduated from high school. It's a little one-story house, more like a bungalow really, but it has a kitchen and a living room and plenty of space for me. I catch a few more hours of sleep after Ethan's interruption and then get up again, ready to enjoy my day off. I grab a beach towel and a Stephen King novel and head from my place down the gravel drive toward my parents' house. The door opens and I head inside, hoping my mom made some bacon or something I can snag before I head to the beach. Even with the amount of time I spend on or near the water doing my job, I can never get enough of being near the ocean. Just as I reach for the pan, my mom emerges out of nowhere and slaps my hand away. The woman is a ninja, I swear to God.

"I'll get you a plate if you're hungry, Tris," she scolds in her patterned apron. "You're not a caveman." She stands nearly six inches under my nose, and I reach over her and snag a muffin before dodging another slap and heading out the door.

As I head toward the beach, I let myself wonder about this Emma girl that Jenny is bringing. My last girlfriend and I had trouble holding a conversation longer than ten minutes. My family would say that I'm a man of few words, though, so maybe it wasn't completely her fault. We just never seemed to have much to talk about. The whole relationship was flat, in retrospect. I don't think either one of us ever really understood the other one, not on a level that mattered. When we broke up I don't think my life even changed. She wasn't in it anymore, but she had been so far on the edge of things already that it just didn't make a huge difference to see her go. I hope my time with Emma is different. I'm not expecting much, especially since I'll only be with her for a few hours at most anyway, but it would still be nice if I could spend that time with someone who I could connect to.

Throughout my whole life, I've been content with what's in front of me. I have my family, and the business we all share, and this town I've grown up in. Ethan left for a while after high school, went to college and traveled a little before coming back. As soon as I graduated I jumped straight into working, and while I don't regret the decision, sometimes I catch myself longing for something new. I find an escape of sorts in my books. I'm the only reader in my family, and if I'm not sailing or surfing then there's a good chance I've got my nose stuck in a horror novel. But the peace that I used to find on the water, in a book or with my family, has become more elusive recently. The waves that I've surfed my whole life are starting to feel stifling. I can't put my finger on what's changed, but I know something has, and it's been getting worse. I pull my old Jeep into the parking lot of the beach that's just a few miles from my house and head toward the water.

There are babies in polka dot suits and sunburned fathers spreading lotion on sunburned kids.

I politely edge past everyone, shaking my head as I go. I make it to the edge of the water and wade out. The water is still cool, but much warmer than it will be once the leaves start turning orange again. I'm used to wearing a full wetsuit when I'm in the sea, but not today. It feels like bath water compared to the normal temperature. I close my eyes and dive in, shutting out the entire world with the sound of the waves.

CHAPTER 6
tristan

By the time the evening rolls around, I'm starting to regret saying yes to Ethan. I need to be ready to go in fifteen minutes and I just finished the Stephen King book I was reading and switched to Tolstoy's *War and Peace*, since my copy of Romeo and Juliet is on hiatus for the time being. The front cover is falling off from me flipping it open too many times. It's my favorite Shakespeare drama, ever since the sixth grade when I was Romeo in a school play. I still know portions of Romeo's part by heart—an embarrassing truth. I stand up, stretching my arms toward the ceiling of my bedroom. It's small, but not so small it's claustrophobic. There's always sand tracked in somewhere from my feet and my bed's almost never made, but it's comfortable. I look at the clock again and start to strip off the swim trunks I'm still wearing while simultaneously looking for a clean pair of jeans.

Like clockwork, Ethan appears in my room at seven forty-five. I almost never bother locking my door, but I start to consider it just to keep him out.

"Let's go, let's go," he says, harassing me as I yank my jeans on. "We're going to be late."

We're not. We live about five minutes from the dock where we're meeting the girls to take them on one of our schooners. I don't bother to argue, just pull on the rest of my clothes and jump into Ethan's truck.

"The sunset is going to be perfect," says Ethan as we speed to the marina. "Not a single cloud."

"I don't think Jenny is going to hook up with you based on the sunset," I answer, and get socked in the arm for my trouble.

He's right, though, for once. The sky is just barely beginning to tinge red and pink as the sun fades.

It all reflects off the water, creating something that looks like two skies on top of the other. We arrive at the dock and Ethan and I clamber out of the truck and he starts to yell something at me as I turn and squint against the glare from the sea. There is Jenny, standing on the dock. She turns and the other girl comes into view and every drop of blood in my veins turns to fire. It's her. It's the girl from the dock.

CHAPTER 7
emma

I'm mortified to be here and I'm sure it's obvious that I'm mortified and that makes it even worse. I'm standing on the edge of the dock with Jenny, who is babbling about how great this date is going to be.

"Ethan has been after me forever," she says, smacking her gum, and I believe it. Jenny has a body like a Greek goddess, with golden hair waving to her shoulders and big brown eyes like a puppy. Everyone likes Jenny. She and I were friends in high school before I moved, even though we were in different grades. Her mother and mine grew up together. She called me the other night and rattled off a story about how she promised a date to this guy and, since the brother was closer to my age, would I come with her since I was in town again? I was a little surprised she called at all, but her and I sometimes hang out when I'm visiting. Still, I politely refused at first. Then I made the mistake of going home and telling my mom about it.

"Emma, of course you should go," she said, conveying total persuasion without raising her voice.

"It's awkward," I argued. "I'm a total third wheel."

"It sounds like you'll be evening out the group, actually," said my mother, the voice of reason.

"There's no way I'm going," I said stubbornly. My mother just smiled.

So, obviously, here I am. She even went through my bags and pulled out a white summer dress and ironed it for me. I insisted on bringing my camera, though. I couldn't resist the shots I could get of the bay at sunset, even if it does make me look like a total weirdo.

My mom and I have been frenzied the last few days, booking guests left and right. She pushed back the first booking dates so we could have a couple of weeks in the house by ourselves, but preparations still need to be done. We've been stocking silver-ware and tablecloths, making sure each room has the right bedding and decorations. Each room has a personality of its own, brought to life with playful seashells in little jars or an elegant lace coverlet. It's been more fun than I expected to help my mom decorate. I might have missed a large portion of the renovations but it makes me feel good to help her choose colors and furniture for every room. My taste runs a little more toward classic than my mom's, but she listens to my opinions and we've settled into a common ground. I forget how quickly my mom and I adjust to each other's wavelengths. She still knows what I'm going to say before I do, and she still has the way of listening to me that makes me feel like she actually cares about every word coming out of my mouth. I'm settling in here, slowly but surely.

Jenny stops in the middle of a sentence and I jolt back to the moment.

"I think they're here," says Jenny, shading her

eyes. I squint as two figures come toward us. As they come closer and are out of the sun's glare, Jenny immediately greets the slightly taller one while the other approaches me. I try to act confident and self-assured but I'm desperately afraid I'm going to somehow manage to fall right off this dock and into the harbor.

"Hi," I say shyly, still shading my eyes. I tuck a loose piece of hair behind my ear. So far, with his back to the sun like that, all I can see is his silhouette.

"Hi," I hear, and he steps directly in front of me, blocking the sunlight from my eyes. I drop my hand.

He's tall, but not too tall. He has hair streaked with blonde, like he spends a lot of time in the sun, and blue eyes as misty as a daydream. He's muscular, with broad shoulders and worn-out jeans that hang on his hips. He runs a hand through his hair as our eyes settle on each other. He stares at me for a quiet second, seemingly unfazed by the silence. His eyes skim over me like I'm a masterpiece he's in the middle of painting, like he's trying to decipher me piece by piece with his gaze. It sounds clinical, but it's not at all, more like looking at a color you've never seen before. I suddenly find it hard to breathe.

"I'm Tristan," he says, finally. Jenny and Ethan are still chatting a few feet from us, oblivious to Tristan and me.

"Emma," I say. I extend my hand out of habit, and he takes it in his and releases it quickly, but the contact sends tremors down the backs of my legs.

"It's nice to meet you," he says quietly. He smiles and I like the way it meets his eyes.

"You, too," I say, smiling.

He somehow makes me feel instantly comfortable and desperately on edge at the same time.

"Are you a photographer?" Tristan asks, nodding at my camera. "That's a nice camera. My brother is always snapping photos and I think he would kill for one like that."

"Yeah, it's amazing," I say, twisting a curl around my fingers.

My camera is my pride and joy, a 35 millimeter Nikon AF. It was expensive, but definitely worth it.

"You should get some great use out of it tonight. It's another great sunset. We should get going before it fades."

We start walking down the dock, heading toward the boat. I toy with the camera strap, winding it around my forearm. I like the fact that Tristan didn't make me feel weird about having it. I hate it when people draw attention to me like that.

"Have you sailed before?" Tristan asks, and I shake my head.

"No," I admit. "I'm a little nervous."

"You're in good hands. Ethan and I have only dumped a tourist into the bay a few times."

I glare at him, but he grins at me so good-naturedly that I smile back.

"I'm joking," says Tristan. "Just wait. You're going to love it."

"Are you guys ready?" Ethan interrupts. "We better go before we lose the wind."

It's blowing hard this close to the water, tangling my hair into knots, but it's still warm enough that I don't feel chilled in my dress and sweater.

Tristan and I both nod and the boys start to lead us over to where the schooner is tied up to the dock. I'm still reeling from this introduction, and I have no idea why. My whole body feels like it's vibrating, and I'm intensely conscious of Tristan's every move. He seems so completely at ease with himself, and something about that steadies me and pulls at me all at once.

We reach the schooner and Tristan hops on easily before turning and reaching a hand out for me. The boat has two masts and looks to be about forty feet long from end to end. I take Tristan's hand and clamber on, bracing myself against his chest as I land. His t-shirt is soft under my fingers, his chest firm. He steadies me politely with a hand at the small of my back. His eyes are smiling.

"Sorry," I say, tilting my chin up toward his face, and he shakes his head.

"Anytime, Emma," he says, ushering me on board. Life jackets are handed out to each of us and I strap mine on, even though it makes me feel like a turtle in a shell.

I feel awkward and clumsy as I head toward the bow, my hair blowing in my face and my feet catching on coils of rope. I settle myself gingerly next to Jenny onto one of the built-in seats—more like a little bench really—and watch the boys get to work. It seems silly that I spent my early life in Rhode Island and never sailed, but it's true. I used to watch boats cross the bay while I stood on the shore, and now I'm finally on one. I'm terrified.

"What's up with you and Tristan?" Jenny asks, turning toward me.

"What do you mean? Nothing's up. We've never met before," I babble like a moron.

Jenny raises an eyebrow. "He was staring at you."

"So?"

"And he was flirting with you."

"Was he?"

Against my will, I feel my cheeks begin to heat. The boys are moving around the boat, discussing things like wind speed and tacking that I don't understand. The final rope is loosened and we begin to glide away from the dock.

"Yeah," says Jenny. "You're sure you've never met him before?"

"I'm sure," I say. The boat is beginning to gain speed and I'm distracted. The boys are still moving in perfect tandem, barking orders to each other, and I wish I understood what was going on or could be of some help, but I know I'd only get in the way. Tristan moves with surprising efficiency and grace under billowing sails, tying off rope ends and moving with assurance across the boat. I watch him in glances, trying to be subtle. Eventually, the wind blows my hair so violently in my face that I turn forward again, and I am dumbstruck. I grab ahold of the rail, pulling myself to my feet even as the wind blows against my body. We're flying over the surface of the water, faster than I could imagine. The waves slap against the body of the schooner but we take them in stride, rising up and over the larger ones.

The sunset turns the water golden, and the light's reflection flashes into my eyes as we skim toward the dark horizon. My nervousness disappears, replaced with the thrill of speed. I grab a railing in each hand

and stand directly at the front of the bow, as far forward as I can get, laughing into the sun. The wind streams through my hair and I feel like I am flying, flying toward the sky. I turn and look back; Jenny is yelling at me from her seat to sit down, Ethan is laughing at Jenny, and Tristan is staring at me across the boat with a gaze so intense it cuts right to my core. I can't stop smiling, enthralled with the sensation of flying. Tristan's lips quirk up, too, after a second, as though he's smiling just because of the stupid grin on my face. Spray from the sea wets my hair and face and I know my cheeks are pink from the sun and the wind. I tear my gaze from Tristan and turn forward again. I could live the rest of my life on this boat, heading toward the horizon and feeling with every second like Earth is farther and farther behind.

CHAPTER 8
emma

We spend another half-hour sailing in the bay, and everyone becomes more relaxed as the night goes on. The boys are laughing and talking with us, although I'm still trying to coax Jenny from where she sits rooted to her seat on the boat. I shoot pictures of everything, nearly falling overboard several times in my quest to get the perfect shot: the sails against the sky, the colors of the sunset, even though I know not even Photoshop will be able to recover the true vibrance of the sky's hues. It gets darker and darker, and the boys turn on a giant spotlight that lights our way. The last rays of sun disappear and the night has been transformed into two skies:

the dark one under the boat and the one glittering with stars above us. Eventually, the boys turn us back toward the harbor.

We head back into the marina, motoring toward the dock, and I've been staring up at the sky for so long I'm getting a kink in my neck. The scattered stars are so bright that it's hard to believe they're real. We bump the wooden edge of the dock gently and Tristan jumps out to tie off the boat. When it's secure, the rest of us climb back onto land, leaving our life jackets on board. The rocking of the dock is so much calmer than being out in open water. The air blowing off the bay chills my sun and wind-burned cheeks.

"Well," says Ethan, "I hope you girls enjoyed yourself."

"Sure," says Jenny, running a hand through her wet hair. "It was fun."

"It was great," I say, shivering a little in my damp dress. "I had a great time."

In the harbor lights I can see Tristan's grin, and the flash of his eyes. I wish I could get a shot of him exactly as he is now, the outline of his silhouette in the dark.

"Didn't your mom drop you off, Emma?" says Jenny, and I nod.

"Yeah," I say. "I'll call her and have her swing by."

"I can take you," says Tristan as he pulls on a jacket. "It's no trouble."

"You don't have to do that," I murmur. I don't want him to feel obligated to take me home or something; this wasn't even a real date.

"It's no trouble," he repeats, grinning down at me. I can't help but smile reluctantly back. The chemistry that's been crackling between us all night returns in full force and I feel it in every inch of me even as I try to ignore it. I know that I just met him—I barely know him—I didn't know it was possible to feel something like this so instantly. I've had a few boyfriends here and there but nothing that really lasted. And nothing that felt like this.

"That's settled, then," says Ethan, beaming. I know he's happy he gets to walk Jenny to her car just the two of them.

We say our goodbyes, and then it's just Tristan and me as we head toward the parking lot. I turn back toward the water one last time, looking at the shifting pattern of the moonlight on the choppy waves.

"I'm glad I got to take you sailing," says Tristan. "I've taken a lot of people on their first trip, but your reaction was by far the best."

"I'm glad you enjoyed it," I say wryly, and he laughs.

"I enjoyed every second," he said. "I've been sailing for so long that I forget what it feels like to be on a boat for the first time. The look on your face was priceless."

I blush, but he says it so honestly that it doesn't make me uncomfortable.

"Have you sailed your whole life?" I ask. He looked like such a natural that I can't imagine otherwise. Tristan directs me toward a Jeep in the parking lot and opens my door for me. I climb in and he shuts it before moving to the other side and getting in the driver's seat. I want to roll my eyes, but the gesture seems so natural to him that I don't have the heart to tease.

"Yeah," he says finally as he starts the car. "My family owns Beyond the Sand, you know, the chartering company. So I learned when I was young. Now I'm out on the water almost every day."

"You're lucky," I say as we start driving. Making small talk with this guy is surprisingly easy. "I'm living in San Diego right now and it's beautiful, in a completely different way."

"I'd love to see California," says Tristan.

"You've never been?"

"Nope. I've lived here all my life. Haven't made it to the west coast."

"Is your whole family here, too?"

Tristan nods, glancing over at me. I can see the outline of his jaw in the flashes of streetlight through the window. Being in a confined space with him is doing something to my insides. He drives with one hand, and for some reason I find that incredibly sexy.

"So your mom owns the bed and breakfast on the cliff?"

I nearly jump at the sound of his voice, and I'm glad he can't see my cheeks flush in the darkness.

"Yeah. It's nearly finished. How did you know that was my mom?"

"Small town," he says, shrugging, and then he sighs. "And I think I saw you standing on the dock the other night, if we're being honest."

"You saw me?"

"Yeah. I was bringing in a tour and happened to glance over in that direction."

He seems a little bashful about it, and I find his shy smile surprisingly attractive.

"So, you were stalking me?"

He laughs, throwing his head back. "Come on," he says. "Give me a little credit. How could I stalk you? I don't even know you."

"I guess I could give you the benefit of the doubt."

He grins at me, and I know the edges of my mouth are turning up at the thought of him noticing me on the dock like that. It sounds a little strange, but it flatters me at the same time. There I was, imagining a ship coming to sweep me away on an adventure, and he was sailing one into the harbor in the fading light. We drive in silence for a second, and instead of feeling awkward, a tension starts to build in the car. I sneak a glance at Tristan and watch his hands flex on the wheel. I grab fistfuls of my sweater but my hands are itching to touch him, and I have no idea why.

"Are you and your mom busy with the bed and breakfast?" asks Tristan, and I'm relieved to have a distraction.

"Yeah," I say, "but we're still getting things ready. We won't have any guests for another week or so."

"So, you're busy but you're not *that* busy."

I hide a smile, still pulling on the hem of my sweater. "I guess you could put it that way."

"Do you want to go out with me tomorrow?"

Tristan pulls the car into the driveway of the inn and parks. I hadn't noticed how close we were to home. He turns toward me, his eyes lit up by the inn's porch lights, looking at me intently. I can't look away, can't even answer. His eyes are so clear in the lights, the rest of his face shaded in darkness. His lips are full and currently serious, the muscles of his jawline flexing as he waits for my answer. I run a hand through my hair and will myself to pull it together. I should say no. I should say no and let this strange night be the end of this encounter between us. I open my mouth to politely refuse.

"Yes," I say, a smile tugging at the corners of my mouth.

I bite my lip to keep from grinning outright. What did I just do?

"Okay, then," says Tristan, smiling at me slowly, and I get the feeling he knows exactly what's been going on in my mind this entire time. I feel totally transparent with him, as though I can't hide anything at all, and I'm not sure I like the sensation. I think he can see every thought running through my head, and I'm not the kind of girl who lays her emotions out to dry on the clothesline for everyone to see. I pull my smile back, biting my lips, and nod.

"I'll pick you up at seven thirty," says Tristan. "If that's alright with you."

"That's fine," is all I say back. We exchange numbers and then I turn to go. But before I can open my door, he has already gotten out of the car and walked around to my side to do it for me. He holds out a hand and helps me out of the Jeep like I'm a princess in a book, and a part of me loves it, but the smarter part of me is beeping a warning.

"Thanks," I say when my feet touch the ground, but he doesn't let go.

"Anytime, Emma," he says, rubbing his thumb across the top of my hand. I let him do it just to show him that he doesn't affect me, and he smiles slowly. My heart is pounding at what feels like a thousand miles per hour.

"I'll see you tomorrow," he finally says, and with that he turns and heads back to the car. He's already back in the driver's seat and pulling away before I start to walk inside. Being near him does things to my mind; he makes it all fuzzy. My hand is still tingling.

CHAPTER 9
emma

I pull open the big oak door as quietly as possible, sneaking in through the smallest crack I can manage.

My mom has left the entryway lights on and I'm walking up the stairs when I hear her voice.

"Ems? Is that you?"

The sound is coming from the parlor, I think. I sigh and return to the bottom step.

"Yeah, it's me," I call. "You didn't have to wait up for me, you know."

My mom removes her reading glasses and closes the book in her lap. She smiles up at me, and I can tell she's tired, but she also looks so happy to see me, as though she's been looking forward to it since I left.

"Your cheeks are all red," she says.

I press my hands to my face self-consciously. "We went sailing," I say.

"On the bay? Wow. That's quite a first date."

"It wasn't a real date, Mom." I am tugging on the hem of my sweater again, which is still damp.

"Right," she says, nodding seriously. "Did you have fun? Were the boys nice?"

"I'm going out with one of them tomorrow," I blurt, spitting the words out quickly, like coals that might burn my tongue. "Tristan. The younger one."

My mom's eyes are dancing, but to her credit she keeps her face perfectly straight. "Well, that sounds nice," she says. "What are you going to wear?"

I laugh out loud, leaning down on my elbows on the back of the couch. "I don't know yet," I say. "I don't think he'll care. Guys never notice what you're wearing."

"The right ones notice everything. I recommend

that pink top you have in your suitcase. Well, it's in your closet now. I hung up all of your clothes."

I'm too tired and too overwhelmed by the night to think about pink tops, or to do anything but shrug helplessly.

"Thanks, Mom," I say, and she squeezes my hand. "I'm going to go to bed."

The moonlight shines through my bay window so brightly that I don't bother turning on a lamp. I could close the blinds, but I don't want to shut out the night. Instead, I go to the little desk by my bed and grab my laptop. It only takes me a second to hook up my camera to the computer. As the photos from tonight upload, flashes of color greet my eyes. Then I sift through them, photo by photo, selecting my favorites, and I start editing. I highlight and darken, focus and crop and move step by step through each picture. I see Tristan's hands on the ropes, the strain of muscle as he fights against an unfurling sail. In each photo I've chosen I see the crook of his smile, the way the wind lifts his hair. Each snapshot of him raises flutters low in my belly. I click through the photos one by one, over and over again, as though tonight was a dream that might slip away in an instant.

CHAPTER 10
tristan

The entire drive home, I hear her voice in my head, her laughter in my ears. I turn up the radio, thinking that music might drown it out, but it makes it worse.

I was not prepared to see her like that. As soon as I saw her, I knew. She turned around on the dock with the colors of the sunset pouring over her like a painting. Her hair was golden and red at the same time, and her eyes—God, her eyes. Pure mermaid eyes, blue with flecks of green, like ocean waves. I thought I was going to make a fool of myself. I was walking toward her before I realized my feet were moving.

And then, on the boat, the way she moved to the bow and held onto the railings, laughing and looking out over the water. She was smiling like she'd never been so happy in her life. I can still see her there, her hair a wild mess, salt spray blasting her every two seconds, and smiling. I watched every move she made—every tilt of her head, every gesture, all night. I couldn't turn away.

I pull into my driveway and switch off the Jeep. The sudden quiet fills my ears and I rub a hand over my face. Tonight was overwhelming. I almost didn't ask her out, thought I could play it cool and just say goodnight. The words were out before I could reason myself out of it. I want to know more about her.

I get out of the Jeep and let myself into my apartment. As soon as I get into the bedroom I strip off my shirt and jeans, which are still damp from the ocean, and turn on the shower in my bathroom. The shower is actually pretty big, with a tiled bench in the corner and enough room so I don't rap my elbows on the walls. I let the hot water run over me and loosen the tight muscles of my back and shoulders, which are tense from sailing. Or maybe it's from being around her all night; I'm not sure. My mind is still full of her. I don't know how I'm going to sleep.

I switch off the water and towel off before yanking on boxers and heading to bed. As I lay down, I lock my hands behind my head and let snapshots of the night flick through my mind: her shy smile in the moment we first met, the sound of her laugh as we rode the waves, the way her cheeks turned red when I asked to see her again. I'm already seeing Romeo and Juliet, Catherine and Heathcliff, and I mentally lock those thoughts down. The last girl I got romantically involved with laughed in my face when I talked about that kind of stuff with her.

"Your head is always stuck in some book," she snorted. "Those characters don't exist in the real world."

And maybe she's right, maybe they don't, but meeting Emma gives me hope. Even if I can't ever tell her, even if I have to lock those feelings down to keep her around and not scare her off the way I did with the last girl, I don't care. I just can't wait to see her again.

CHAPTER 11
tristan

The next morning, I wake up wondering if it was all a dream.

I lean over to check my phone on the nightstand but there are no texts or calls. I roll to my back, staring at the ceiling. What the hell am I going to do until seven-thirty tonight? It's barely five-thirty in the morning now, but I'm wide awake and I don't have a tour until ten, and even that will only take a few hours.

I roll out of bed and pull on sweatpants, walking right past the little kitchen in my apartment. With my mom cooking right next door, most of the time my kitchen goes unused.

I open the back door and head straight into the kitchen. My mom isn't awake yet so I grab a loaf of bread and stick a couple pieces in the toaster. I'm reaching for the milk when I hear the sound of shuffling slippers.

"You're up early, Tris. I thought you didn't have a tour until later."

My mom is wearing the same bathrobe I can remember her having since I was only twelve years old; I think it was red and white originally, like a candy cane, but the red has faded to pink over the years.

"I woke up early," I say. "Couldn't sleep."

"You got in a little late, too, didn't you?"

"What are you, a ninja?"

"I'm your mother. I know these things."

"I wasn't in that late."

"Did you have a good time on your date?" She looks at me innocently.

"Yeah, actually. I did."

"Really?"

She is making coffee now, trying to downplay

her interest, but I know she's dying to know what happened. She's been waiting for Ethan or me to get married since we were old enough to propose.

"Yes, Mom. And that's all I'm saying about it."

I grab my toast and glass of milk and head for the door. I can't talk about Emma with my mom yet.

"Wait! Tristan, wait."

She follows me to the back door, all pretense of nonchalance slipping away, and I can't help but grin.

"At least tell me one thing about her. Only one, and I swear I won't ask anything else."

"Jeez, Ma. I just met her last night."

"Well what is she like?"

"She's . . . " I shrug my shoulders, at a total loss. "I don't know. But I do know I'm not coming in to make toast tomorrow morning."

My mother ignores this jab. "Did you like her? Was she funny, smart?"

"She's perfect, Ma."

I open the door and head back toward my

apartment, shaking my head. My mom is still standing at the back door, hand pressed to her heart, when I shut the door behind me.

CHAPTER 12
tristan

Despite my impatience, the rest of the day flies by. I do my tour and come back home to stick my nose back in *War and Peace*. In the afternoon I help out with some boat repairs. I'm handy with pretty much anything, and there's always something that needs fixing on one of our boats. After that, I make sure that everything will be perfect for tonight. A part of me worries I'm wasting my time. Even *War and Peace* isn't enough to distract me from the nagging anxiety that I made some mistake. As seven thirty draws closer I worry that she's actually boring, and spending an evening with her will be nothing like what I expect.

But what do I expect? I ask myself as I head to her house. I have a tendency to make things up in my head, to think that everything is going to end up the way it does in one of my books. I probably imagined whatever connection I thought I had with her. That seems much more likely than believing what I experienced last night is real. Already prepared to chalk the night up to a total loss, I pull into the gravel drive of the bed and breakfast. The sun isn't quite yet setting behind the white boards and brick. I'm excited to get onto the water if nothing else. I open the Jeep door and hop down, inhaling deeply. It smells like fresh-cut grass and ocean spray. I can't help but admire the inn and its location—Emma is lucky to have a place like this. I see the little sign bearing her name and smile as I start toward the door. She sounded so wistful last night when she asked about my family, but from what I can see she has a mother who loves her a lot. I'm about to jump the porch steps when the front door opens.

She's wearing a pink dress the same color as the blush on her cheeks, and I've never seen pink look so good on a girl before. Her hair shines golden and her eyes are bright and clear. Everything I felt last night rushes back, and I know I wasn't wrong to ask her out tonight. She is still standing there on the porch, smiling at me with an eyebrow raised quizzically.

"What?" she says.

"Nothing," I say, snapping out of it. "You look gorgeous."

Her cheeks turn a darker shade of pink, and she tilts her head forward so her hair falls in a cascade around her face, like she's trying to hide.

"Ready?" I ask.

"I don't even know where we're going."

"I thought we could go on the water again, if you wanted to."

I watch her eyes light up and I know I made the right choice in planning the date.

"Perfect," she says, stepping down the porch stairs. She's wearing a light sweater over her dress and as she walks toward me it slips off one shoulder. I find it incredibly distracting. As we walk the few steps to the car I catch her scent and it turns me inside out. It smells floral and musky, with a hint of what I'm starting to recognize as just Emma. I open the door for her and she climbs in carefully. She has these shoes on, not really heels but they have a heel? Anyways, she's treating them with caution. They make her legs look about a mile long. I grin, wondering if she wore them for me. I hope so.

CHAPTER 13
tristan

"Are we going on the same boat as last night?" she asks as soon as I start the car. She sounds bubbly and excited and I find it intoxicating.

"No," I say, smiling at her. "We're taking *Dolphin*, one of the charter yachts."

"You're taking me on a yacht?"

I laugh, knowing she's picturing some four-story-high floating concoction that's essentially a house on the water.

"Not the way you're thinking," I say. "It's smaller than that. It's motorized so I don't have to spend so much time manning it as I would if we were sailing.

But there's a furnished cabin, a bed and everything, so it's more comfortable than a schooner."

"I liked the schooner," says Emma.

"Trust me," I say. "This will be even better."

"I trust you," she says quietly, and the words make my stomach leap. I care about what this girl thinks of me, and I've known her for barely twenty-four hours. She glances at me and I get a glimpse of those mermaid eyes. They are just as I remember: blue and green swirled in a perfect mix like a tropical lagoon. I could get lost in her eyes. With an effort, I bring my attention back to the moment.

"Why didn't you bring your camera with you tonight?" I ask, glancing at her empty hands.

"I have it in my purse," she admits, giggling again. "I knew it was geeky but I couldn't resist. The light on the bay is so perfect right now."

"I don't think it's geeky," I say, driving toward the harbor. "Seriously. Did you look at any of the pictures you took last night?"

"Yes," she answers. "I uploaded them all to my computer, I even did some editing."

"Any good ones?"

"A few. Maybe you can see them on our next date." She grins at me from the passenger's seat and I realize I like her teasing me. She's a little shy and so sweet that even when she's teasing she does it hesitantly, like she's trying to make sure she doesn't hurt my feelings.

"If I'm lucky?"

"Yes."

We're already talking about our next date as though it's set in stone. But the weird part is that I'm not freaked out. It feels comfortable. We're in the parking lot of the harbor before I realize it, and I jump out and get Emma's door. She reaches for my hand but I remember her heels, so I reach up and take her by the waist and set her down gently on her two feet. She falls against me as she lands, and having her so close nearly puts me over the edge. Her scent washes over me before she steps back and I'm left standing alone, so turned on it's hard to breathe.

"Let's go," I say, and reach for her hand. After a

second of hesitation, she takes it. I brush my thumb over her skin and she exhales a long, shaky breath; I enjoy the moment of hope that she might be as affected by me as I am by her. The thought is exhilarating, but completely frightening at the same time. We head toward the marina, walking along the dock until we come to *Dolphin*. It's similar in size to the schooner, but more maneuverable. Emma's face is already lighting up at the prospect of being on the water again. She hops right onto the deck, already exploring.

"Don't go into the cabin yet," I call to her, fiddling with the ropes. "Stay on the deck."

"Why?" she yells back.

"Because I said so," I say. I want to see her face when she walks in.

I can hear her huff out an impatient breath and I smile.

"Okay, come on," I call, and Emma appears from the side of the boat and waits at the door with me. Her sweater is still slipping off her shoulder and I fight the urge to nudge it the rest of the way down myself. Instead, I open the cabin door and enjoy the sight of her mouth dropping open.

The cabin is pretty standard, with side couches, a tiny kitchen, and a bedroom at the back. And it's not really a bedroom, just a bed in a room with a porthole overlooking the water. In the front is the bridge: steering wheel, radio, navigation system, and power controls. I move over there and switch on the motor. It purrs to life, and I complete my safety check of all the dials before heading back outside to untie us.

Back inside the bridge, I take the wheel and guide us out of the marina. Emma walks straight to the front window.

"Holy shit," she breathes, and I laugh out loud.

"Pretty sweet, huh?" I ask, guiding the boat out into the harbor. The sound of the motor hums in my ears and vibrates my seat, and the color of the sunset blazes in through the front window.

"I think it is," says Emma. "You get to go out on these things every day?"

"Not every day," I answer. "But *Dolphin* is one of my favorites."

Emma grins, still staring out the front window. We leave the marina and the no-wake zone and I aim straight out into Narragansett Bay.

"Are you hungry?" I ask. We never really talked about what this date would entail, but I made sure *Dolphin* was ready for anything.

"Not really," she says. "Maybe a little. Why?"

"Open the fridge."

She goes straight to the little fridge and peeks in. I've stocked it with strawberries and Hershey's chocolate bars, some sandwiches, and a bottle of champagne.

"Did you do this?" she asks, staring inside the fridge.

"Yup," I say. "I wanted you to have chocolate-covered strawberries but it was too late to order some. Chocolate bars and strawberries were the best I could do. And sandwiches because they're the only thing I can make."

She is staring at me with a grin on her face that's

impossible not to love. "It's perfect," she says, still smiling. "It's really nice, Tristan. I wasn't expecting this at all."

"It's just sandwiches and chocolate bars," I answer. "I wanted to do something for you."

She walks toward me slowly, until her face is inches from mine, framed by the sunset.

"It's perfect," she says again, quietly. "Thank you."

"You're welcome," I say, reaching for her hand. I can't think about anything but how close she is and how good she feels against me. Her arms twine around my shoulders and I still my hands on her hips. She's like smoke under my hands, like if I hold her too tightly she'll disappear through my fingers. But the longer she's pressed against me the harder she is to resist. She pulls away suddenly, grabs her camera, and steps outside. I turn my attention back to steering the boat, grinning like an idiot.

"I'm going to take some shots of the water," stammers Emma. Her cheeks are flushed but she's fighting a smile. All I can do is grin stupidly back at her as she heads toward the bow. It's like we're both feeling the same thing, and my gut flutters with nerves and anticipation. I can't believe I get to spend the entire evening with her.

"Do you want to stop for a while?" I call after a few minutes. We're pretty far from the marina now, in the open water of the bay. The wind is warm, and the bay is calmer than I've ever seen it, just miles of quiet water.

"Sure," she calls back, and I shut off the motor. The boat rocks gently as I wander outside to the deck. Emma is standing at the very front of the bow, looking back at me. The bay is dotted with other boats, but we're far enough from them to have privacy. Her camera is in her hands.

Emma sighs, the wind in her hair. "This is so beautiful," she says. "I would love to be able to do this everyday."

"You want to drive and sail tourists around the bay every day?"

She laughs, shaking her head. "No, I guess not.

But I would love to have this kind of canvas to shoot everyday."

"Do you do a lot of photography in San Diego?"

Her shoulders hunch forward as she frames a few shots of the water.

"Not really," she admits. "I worked as a waitress all last year but didn't take a lot of photos, even in my spare time."

"Why not? There's gotta be pretty nice sunsets in SoCal too, right?"

"Yeah, they're beautiful. But my dad never really got the whole photography thing."

"Did you choose not to pursue it because of him?"

She frowns, and a shadow crosses her face. "Sort of," she says. "But I could have done it when I moved to San Diego, and I didn't, so I'm not sure I can blame it all on him. Part of it was me, too, somehow."

"What do you mean?"

"I'm not sure. Maybe I just started to believe what he was saying, that there was no point in me pursuing it at all."

"Do you still believe that?"

"I don't know."

I nod, not wanting to push her any farther. "You live with your dad most of the time?"

"Yeah. He's in Massachusetts. I moved to San Diego with a few friends after high school."

"Do you miss him when you're here?"

"Yeah. But it's nice being on my own, too. And it's great being with my mom, being where I grew up."

I catch an edge of sadness in her voice. I admire her moving to San Diego on her own, but it's not something I'd ever want to do. Even with her friends, it sounds like she's lonely. I shift so that I'm standing behind her, my hands stuffed in my pockets. Emma presses her back into my chest, and leans her head against my shoulder. I stand still, afraid that if I move I'll scare her away again.

"Do you want to swim?" I ask.

"Seriously?" she turns toward me, finally. I've wanted to look at those eyes all night.

"Yeah, seriously."

"It's freezing! And is it even safe to swim out here? We're in the middle of the ocean."

I laugh, throwing my head back. "It's summertime," I say. "The bay is as calm and warm as it ever gets. And we're not in the middle of the ocean. It's not dangerous."

"What if we get run over?"

"By all the boats?" I wave my hands around for effect; there isn't another vessel anywhere near us.

She folds her arms, looking stubborn. "I don't have a suit," she says

I grin at her. "Who says you're going to need one?"

Her mouth drops open and her cheeks immediately flush red, and I start to laugh before she can say a word.

"I'm kidding, I'm kidding," I say, smiling at her. I hope she's not seriously offended. But she looks so cute when she's embarrassed

"Quit teasing me," she says, a smile playing with the edges of her lips.

"I'm sorry," I say, still grinning.

"No you're not."

"Sure I am."

I step toward her. She meets my gaze for a second but then turns back toward the water.

"I don't know if I want to swim," she says.

I don't think she's really annoyed, she's just nervous, and now I feel bad for putting her on edge. "We definitely don't have to if you don't want to," I say, running a hand through my hair. "It's up to you. It was just an idea."

"Do you have extra suits on board somewhere?"

"Yeah, in the bedroom closet."

"I'll change first, and then you can." She flashes me a quick smile and I grin back.

Well, well, well. Seems like she's full of surprises.

When Emma walks out of the bedroom all I can do is stare. She has chosen a black one-piece with cutouts on the sides and a plunging back.

"Your turn," she says quietly, and I quickly enter and change into blue swim trunks. When I come out again, Emma is back at the front rail of the bow.

She has long legs made even longer by the way she's balanced up on her toes like a ballerina.

"Why are you standing like that?" I ask, grinning.

"My feet are cold," she says, smiling back at me as the wind blows her hair back from her face. "We better do this now before I lose my nerve."

I lead her to the ladder on the side of the boat but then change my mind.

"Here," I say, leading her to the side of the cabin, where there is a ladder to the roof. "We can climb up here and jump off."

"What?"

"Are you afraid? It's not that far."

She frowns at me, glancing from the water to the cabin and back again.

"Emma," I say quietly, and her eyes snap to mine. "Trust me," I say, and her breathing slows. She's seemed a little on edge all night but now, with her eyes locked on mine, she settles.

"Okay," is all she whispers, and with a small smile she puts her hand in mine and I lead her to the short ladder and we climb the top of the cabin. Emma is grinning now, all trace of hesitation gone, and I take her hand in mine again.

"Are you ready?" I ask, and she nods quickly, her little hand squeezing mine so hard it's about to cut off my circulation. "On three," I say. "One, two . . . "

She yanks me with her as she leaps off the top of the cabin, and we're airborne for a full second before we plunge into the Atlantic. Cold, gray water closes over us, and I kick back to the surface, shaking the water out of my eyes. It's so warm outside that the cold water feels good. Emma pops up next to me, brushing her hair out of her eyes. She's smiling but her teeth are already starting to chatter.

"Too cold?" I say, swimming to her. I grab for her hand and she smiles. We are both breathing hard from the cold and the work of staying afloat.

"You're shivering," I say.

"I'm okay," she says, kicking her way closer to me. I swim us over to the boat and nudge her toward the railing. She reaches up and climbs the ladder, and all the blood drains out of my head as I watch her.

She has the most perfect body, with those long legs and her hair plastered against her skin and shining like wet copper. I pull myself up after her, darting into the cabin for towels. I wrap the biggest one I can find around Emma, rubbing her shoulders until she stops quivering. She smiles up at me, looking more relaxed than she has all night, and I smile down at her.

"Are you hungry?" I ask.

She nods. "A little," she says, wringing her hair out with the towel. "Those strawberries are starting to sound pretty good."

"Come on," I say, leading her back into the cabin. She plops down on one of the side benches and twirls her wet hair into a bun on the top of her head. It makes me smile; all that work doing her hair for this date, and now it's ruined. I love the fact that she doesn't seem to mind. I think she looks as gorgeous with soaking wet hair piled into a bun as she did at her doorstep.

"What are you smiling about?" she asks me softly.

"I was thinking how beautiful you look," I answer

honestly. A smile tilts the corners of her mouth as she gazes at me, but she still looks guarded. A shield comes down over her face right as it looks like she's about to let me in. It's frustrating, and I don't know how to break through it but I know I'll keep trying. She completely intrigues me, and with every piece of her she lets slip through the cracks I like her more and more. She has a sweetness to her that gets to me in a way I didn't expect. I open the fridge and pull out strawberries and the chocolate bars and the bottle of champagne. It's nothing fancy, but I thought she might like it.

"Do you want a sandwich?" I ask.

She shakes her head. I pour two glasses of the champagne and set everything down on the little table in front of the bench and then sit across from Emma.

"Aren't you cold?" she asks, wrapped in her towel, but I shake my head. Just being this close to her has me so worked up I feel like I need to go dip my head again. She glances up at me, taking a tiny bite of a strawberry, and my blood pressure spikes.

"So you and your family run this whole business?" she asks.

"Yup. Me and my dad and brother. My mom handles most of the paperwork."

"That's pretty amazing, all of you working together like that."

Again, the tone of sadness.

"Yeah, it's pretty great," I answer, shrugging. "I want to kill Ethan some days and I know my mom wants to kill all of us most of the time, but we make a pretty good team."

She nods, looking down at the table. I want to move over there and hold her but I lock my hands together, telling myself to be patient.

"Were you singing on the dock the night I saw you?" I ask, and her head comes up.

"Yeah, I was," she admits, laughing, and for a moment the shield drops. "I can't believe you heard that."

"The wind must have been blowing in my direction," I answer, grinning. "That, and mermaids always sing."

"What?"

Now I'm flustered.

"You, uh," I stammer. "I guess you reminded me of a mermaid, the way you were poised out there on the dock, singing. Legend has it mermaids used to lure sailors to their death with their songs."

"I guess I should expect you to be familiar with ocean lore, since you've been a sailor your whole life," says, Emma, smiling, and I'm relieved she doesn't seem to think I'm a total weirdo. "And I'm no mermaid. It was just a lullaby my mom used to sing to me."

The champagne is starting to make her cheeks flush, and it's fucking adorable.

"My mom didn't really sing for us," I say. "But she played a lot of AC/DC, REO Speedwagon. But she loved country, too. I know every Dixie Chicks song because she had total control of the stereo in our house and I had no choice."

Emma is laughing, spilling drops of her champagne as her body shakes.

"That's amazing," she says, and I'm already walking over to the command center and turning the radio on, picking out a CD. I turn on "Keep On Lovin' You" by REO Speedwagon and as the sound fills the cabin I walk back over to Emma and hold out my hand. She bites her lip but sets her glass down and stands up, taking my hand. I take her left hand in mine and take her waist in my right, pulling her close. Her entire back is bare from the cut of the suit and her skin is warm and silky under my hands. She glances up at me, her cheeks flushed and her lips parted. I grin down at her and she smiles hesitantly as I start to move, leading us around the limited space of the cabin. She loosens up and leans into me as we dance, the song playing in the background.

Her head fits perfectly tucked under my chin, and as she lies against my chest I hope she doesn't hear how fast my heart is beating. I hold her close to me, caressing her back, and her muscles tense under my touch. Her wet hair smells like salt water and that floral scent that clings to her skin. She links her hands around my waist, and her back arches. She tilts her face toward mine, and our eyes connect. I take her chin in my hand and kiss her the way I've wanted to since I saw her standing on the dock at sunset. Her lips are soft and warm and she tastes like champagne and the sea. Her mouth opens and the heat is so sudden that I almost lose control. I feel someone quiver and I have no idea which one of us it is.

She yanks away from me. "I can't," she says, and I can see she's trembling. Her eyes are huge. Her chest is rising and falling as fast as mine.

"I'm sorry," I say. "I'm sorry, I thought—"

"It's not your fault," she says. "I wanted to. I just . . . I can't."

"Emma, what's wrong?"

I take a step toward her and she backs away, raising her hands to ward me off.

"Don't," she says, and the tremble in her voice tears a hole in my chest. I have no idea what is the matter but I can tell she's shutting down.

"Did I do something?" I ask.

"No," she says. "You didn't. This is my fault."

She finally meets my eyes and she looks miserable, completely torn. I wish she would open up to me and tell me what is going on in her head, but as she folds her arms across her stomach I know she won't. The cabin is silent except for the soft hush of lapping waves. I don't want our date to be over, but I can't bear to see her so uncomfortable.

"Do you want me to take you home?" I ask quietly.

Her eyes snap to mine. She nods and wraps herself tightly in the towel again, turning away from me.

CHAPTER 14
tristan

It's a quiet trip back to the dock, and when we arrive Emma jumps out and heads right to the car while I tie up. When I let myself into the truck and start the engine, Emma turns to the window.

The drive back to Emma's house is so quiet that I can hear my blood pounding in my ears. Emma is back in her pink dress and sweater, toying with the hem and staring out the window. She looks miserable and I feel awful. Half of me regrets kissing her, and half of me would do it over again in a heartbeat. I run a hand over my hair, wishing I could take her hand but not wanting to make her any more upset. I don't know what made her react the way she did, but we're not going to get anywhere if she won't even talk to me about it. My hands flex on the wheel over and over again as we finally pull into her driveway. The edges of the drive are lined with lights that flicker in the dark and make shadows over Emma's skin. My throat is tight; I don't want to let her go. I don't know her yet, but I want to. And now I'm worried I might never get the chance. I put the Jeep in park and we sit for another moment in silence. I can hear crickets chirping outside in the dark, and the sound of Emma's breathing.

"I guess I should go," she finally says. Her voice is small and so quiet I almost miss it.

"I don't want you to," I answer, and she shakes her head slowly. She won't meet my eyes. "But if that's what you want, or what you think is best, I guess you should go. I just wish I knew why you feel that way."

She looks over at me and it's like looking into a wall. She's not giving an inch. She opens the car door herself for the first time and shuts it gently behind her before she walks away. I start the car again and drive off before I have a chance to jump out and demand she tell me what's going on in her head. With every foot I put between us I feel more and more stupid. Images flash into my mind from the evening we spent together: her hand in mine as we jumped off the boat, her hair blowing in the wind, her face when I made her laugh. I thought maybe, this time, it would be real, that she felt the same connection I did. But it looks like I was wrong about her. It looks like I was wrong about everything.

CHAPTER 15

emma

I listen to the sound of his wheels spinning on the gravel as he leaves, and the tightness in my chest worsens with every step I take. I pull my sweater tighter around my torso with shaking hands as I walk toward the house. I can still feel his hands on my skin, like his fingertips branded me with a secret code. His eyes after I pulled away from him were a dark blue, burning into mine, but as soon as he realized I was upset they widened with concern. And when he kissed me, oh God, when he kissed me. There was so much heat—it got too intense too quickly. I couldn't handle it, couldn't handle the way it felt. It was like all of me was slowly pouring into him with every second we were connected. It scared me so badly that I ran. I ran, and now here I am with this ache in my chest that won't go away. I rub a hand over my heart as I open the front door, slip inside, and shut it behind me. I lean against the heavy wood and slide down until I am sitting on the foyer rug, my back pressed against the door. I rub my temples with my fingers and fight the tears that I know are coming. I'm an idiot. I'm such an idiot. But how was I supposed to know he would bring me strawberries and Hershey bars and tell me I was beautiful?

I hear footsteps and I brush away my tears with the backs of my hands, knowing she'll notice anyway.

"Emma?" My mom walks down the stairs and stops on the bottom step. "What's wrong?"

"Nothing," I say, but my voice wobbles and gives me away.

"Did something happen? Are you alright?"

"I'm fine."

There is an awkward pause and my tears start

flowing again, unchecked. She knows I'm lying and I know I'm lying but I'm so humiliated by the way I left, I can't bring myself to tell her what's going on.

"Emma, it's okay." Her voice is soothing, and as she leans down to lay a hand on my knee I see the concern in her eyes. All I can do is shake my head, grateful when all she does is kneel next to me and doesn't ask any more questions. A part of me wants to talk, just to get it all out so it will stop weighing me down, but the words won't come. I struggle to my feet and my mom does the same.

"I'm going to bed," I say, and her face falls. Her hands lock together, her fingers interlacing. Before she can convince me to stay, to tell her what happened and let her help, I bolt up the stairs. The door to my room is already open. I close it behind me and drop onto my bed, sobbing.

Even as the hours go by, I can't sleep. I shower and change into PJs but I'm not any more comfortable. I sit curled up like a cat in my window seat, looking out over the sea. Everything is dark, and the crescent moon shimmers on the waves. I'm exhausted, but I can't sleep. Every time I close my eyes I see him, hear his voice. I ran because I was afraid, but I'm even more afraid to tell him I wish I hadn't. My knowledge of love is limited to slamming doors and screams, and the sound of someone crying when they think everyone else is asleep. It's strange how things like that affect you even when you do everything you can to forget. I turn my phone over and over again in my hands, wishing he would call and hoping he won't. I curl my bare toes under the blanket I'm wrapped in. I have all this tension bottled up somewhere in my chest and I don't know how to release it. I twist my phone in my hands and look up at the star-strewn sky, and I press his name with my thumb.

The phone rings and it shocks me so much that I immediately hang up, cursing myself for being a coward. I brace myself and try again, my anxiety level growing with every ring. He's probably sleeping. He's probably sleeping or out having a good time or doing something that involves not caring at all that I ran out on our date. I shouldn't wake him. I should just hang up now.

"Hello?"

His voice is rough with sleep, and so sexy it makes my stomach flip and roll.

"Hi," I say, and I hear him let out a slow breath.

"Emma," he says, his voice still low, and everything inside me yearns at the sound of my name coming out of his mouth.

"I'm sorry," I whisper, fighting tears for the thousandth time tonight. "I'm sorry. I shouldn't have run."

"It's okay," he says. I hear the rustle of blankets as he sits up. I wonder what he's wearing, if he's wearing anything, and my face immediately begins to heat.

"It's okay?" I repeat, incredulous. "It's not okay. I left like a moron in the middle of our date, I was rude to you, I—"

"It's okay," he says again, his voice warming, and I am humbled.

"I thought you would be angry," I say honestly.

"I was, a little. More like frustrated."

"Why aren't you mad now?"

"Because I heard your voice."

I stretch out my legs so the adrenaline will have somewhere to flow in my veins. My heart flutters like a bird in a cage.

"Can I see you?" I say.

I swear I can hear him smile.

"Do you want me to drive over there?"

"Yeah," I say, laughing. I cover my mouth with my hand, but I am exhilarated. "Come over. Just for a minute."

"I'm coming. Watch for my lights."

"Okay."

I hear the click of the line and I spring up, looking for something cuter to throw on than my baggy pajama pants. My hair is still drying in curls down my back but at least it's clean. I pull on my softest pajama bottoms and a pale green top that skims the top of my hips, wishing I still had some of my makeup on. Just as I'm yanking on shoes I see the lights of his Jeep pull around the curve of the driveway. I open my bedroom door and sneak down the stairs as quietly as I possibly can, skidding to a stop at the braided rug in front of the door. I slip out the door through the smallest crack I can manage and shut it silently behind me, and then I am flying, running toward the lights as fast as I can. I am smiling so big it's hurting my face. He turns off the headlights and opens the driver's side door and steps out to meet me.

I don't stop. I run straight into his arms, and he wraps them around me in the same instant, cupping the back of my head with his hands. I tuck my head right under his chin, where it was when we were dancing. His hands move over my back in slow, soothing circles, and my breaths begin to calm. He smells of sleep and some kind of soap and the combination makes my pulse flutter. When my breathing has settled, I tilt my face up to his, a brave move that gives me a little jolt of fear. His eyes meet mine and his lips curve up in a smile as he leans down and kisses my jawline so lightly it might have just been the night air. He travels along to my chin and to the other side of my face, brushing kisses along my skin, and I reach my hands up his back and grip his shoulders. It's all rushing back, the same emotions I was feeling on the boat. This time I don't run. I let them flood through me and I trust him just enough to stay where I am. He moves his hands to my face and runs them through my hair and I catch his lips with mine and finally, finally, he kisses me.

His lips are soft and strong and all I can think about is how much I don't want this to stop. He pulls back, nips my lower lip and then kisses it softly, like an apology. I can feel how hard he's breathing and I know my chest has to be rising and falling as quickly as his. I wrap my arms around his neck, pressing myself as close to him as I can get. We've come to rest against the side of the Jeep, my back to the metal door. His lips nudge mine open and his tongue strokes mine, slow and soft and warm all at the same time. His hands slide to my hips and start to knead and my body is writhing beneath his touch. I want more, so much more, and that's when I break away.

"Hold on," I say, barely recognizing my own breathy voice. He leans his forehead against mine. I try to get my breathing under control.

"Hi, by the way," says Tristan, and I giggle.

"Hi," I say, and he runs one of his hands through my hair.

"I'm glad you called."

"I am, too."

"I'm really sorry," I say. "I shouldn't have done that to you."

"I thought you hated me."

"I didn't hate you. I had a great time. I just, I don't know, I freaked out."

"You had a great time?"

His voice is so hopeful, like a little kid who's been told he can have another piece of candy, and it makes me smile.

"Yeah, of course I did. It was amazing."

"Then why did you run?"

I step a few inches away from him and the car,

considering his question, but he won't let go of my hand. I find it very hard to concentrate when we're close to each other. I want to open up to him, but what I'm feeling is so new that I'm not sure where to start. And I've still only known him for two days.

"I got scared," I say. I'm repeating myself, but it's true. "I was having such a good time and, I don't know. I let my guard down with you and it scared me."

"It doesn't have to scare you," Tristan says in a low voice. "I would never hurt you."

"You can't know that," I protest. "There's no way you can make that promise."

Tristan shrugs and grins at me, and I know his mind is made up. But I've seen what can happen when two people break that promise. I know that nothing is set in stone, not even love. Especially not love.

"Can we just agree to take this slowly?" I ask, running a hand through my hair. Tristan steps toward me, maneuvering me back to where I was and I ward him off before he can touch me and ruin my train of thought.

"I mean," I continue, "I'm only here for the summer, until the end of August."

He nods, leaning toward me, and my rational thought is slipping away. My back is pressed to the Jeep and I have nowhere to run, even though a growing part of me doesn't want to go anywhere. As Tristan's hands come around my waist I press my hand to his chest.

"I know what you're going to say," says Tristan before I can open my mouth. "And I hear you loud and clear. I know you're not here forever, I know we just met and we don't know what the hell is happening between us. But I'm not going to walk away now just because of all the reasons we should."

"Why?"

He strokes my cheekbone with his thumb, and my lips fall open.

"Because you're beautiful when you smile. And I want to know more about you; I want to know everything about you. And because our chemistry is off the charts."

"I'm not sure about that."

He leans in and proves me a liar. My lips open with a sigh and I grab fistfuls of the front of his shirt and lose myself. I am on my tiptoes, reaching as high as I can, trying to get closer to him. He wraps both hands in my hair and pulls my head back and before I can do anything but obey he starts kissing his way from my jaw down my neck. He swirls his tongue into the hollow of my collarbone and I shiver before he straightens and claims my lips again. I am out of excuses and escape plans, but it's he who stops us this time. As he pulls his mouth from mine I'm aware of the intense ache between my legs, and the bulge in his sweatpants. Tristan puts his hands on either side of my head and leans in, his face inches from mine. He's wearing a t-shirt, and as he leans toward me I admire the ripple of his shoulder muscles. His body is muscular, but streamlined, with wide shoulders and narrow hips. He stands so far above me that I have to tilt my head to look him in the eye, but I don't mind. For once, I'm okay with the idea of being the fragile one and letting him protect me. I have the strangest feeling that he actually would, that I can trust him. I pull myself back. It's too early to know anything for sure. Tristan kisses the tip of my nose, pulling me from my thoughts.

"I can see those wheels turning in your head," he says, and I can't even protest. The guy's only known me for two days but apparently I'm transparent to him.

"Just relax," he continues. "You have nothing to worry about." He folds me in his arms, just holds me, and I wrap my arms around his waist and let him comfort me. The stress and embarrassment from tonight fades away and I let myself enjoy being held by someone who seems to actually care about me. Tristan kisses my forehead, then my temple and my cheek, and I smile up at him.

"I better get home," he says. "Before your mom comes out here and kicks my ass."

"She would, too," I answer, and he laughs.

"If she's anything like you, I believe that," he says. "Do you want me to walk you to the door?"

I love that he's such a gentleman and thinks about things like that.

"No, I'm fine," I say. "If we extend this good-bye any longer you might not make it home before morning."

"That doesn't sound too bad to me," he whispers, leaning in to kiss my neck, and my whole system jolts alive again. He grins at me, kisses me quick and hard twice more and then opens the door of his Jeep.

My body already feels cold, bereft without him. He waves at me through the window and then pulls out of the drive, and I watch his lights fade away into the distance before I start walking back to the house. I press my hands to my swollen lips, my hot cheeks. I can barely believe the turn this night has taken. Was I seriously sitting in my room and crying two hours ago?

I run a hand through my hair and spin in a circle. The stars blink down on me, bright and silent. I feel so completely alive. I might not be ready for anything too serious, but a little excitement can't hurt anything, right? After the way tonight ended up, I'm not sure I could stay away from Tristan if I tried, and I obviously don't want to.

I sneak back into the house inch by inch, praying I don't hit a squeaky step. I make a mental note to apologize to my mom in the morning. She didn't deserve for me to come home upset and snap at her for being worried. We spend so much time apart, but after a few days with her all the easiness of our relationship starts flooding back. She wanted me to go to college here, but I took a year off to try and decide what I wanted. I sigh as I climb the stairs to my room.

The only thing I've ever really wanted to do for the rest of my life was photography, but my dad is completely against the idea. That was why I left in the first place, but here I am a year later and I still haven't made any progress at making a career out of it.

I push the thoughts from my mind as I crawl

into bed, pulling my quilts into a cocoon. I lie on my side, looking out the window, and wonder what Tristan is thinking right now. I hope his body is aching the way mine is; I hope he's thinking about me, too.

I melt into my pillows and start to drift off immediately. It's been such a long day that my body and my mind have been on complete overload. The last thing in my mind before I drift off is Tristan's body pinning me to the side of the Jeep, and the way his eyes softened when I ran into his arms.

CHAPTER 16

emma

I wake up the next morning slowly, like always, stretching my arms above my head and burying my head under my pillow before lifting it an inch. I peek out at the sun coming in through my window and wonder if last night was all a dream. It seems like it was, but it's too clear. It was real.

I sit up and grope wildly for my phone even though I know it's too early for him to have texted me, but something pops up.

Want breakfast? I've got muffins if you're interested.

I can't believe he already texted me. Isn't there some unwritten rule that guys are supposed to try and act cool after dates and not text girls for a few days? If there is, I'm glad Tristan broke it. I type back a quick message:

Muffins sound good

He replies almost instantaneously:

Disclaimer, I had a bite of yours. Be at your house in five.

I am grinning like an idiot.

I watch Tristan pull into my driveway and yank my sandals onto my feet. I'm a mass of nerves and I can feel my entire body starting to tremble at the thought of seeing him again. I keep trying to clear my head, but it's becoming impossible—he's taken up residence there and won't get out. I descend the stairs two at a time and dart out the front door, hoping to leave before my mom has time to ask questions. I run to his Jeep and throw the door open, launching myself inside, and wind up nearly in Tristan's lap.

"Sorry," I say, breathing hard, but Tristan is already laughing. He takes my chin in his hand and kisses me softly, and I let out a slow breath. He releases my chin and kneads the back of my neck in a way that makes me sigh, and then pulls away.

"Hi," he says softly, his eyes a misty blue.

"Hi," I say back. "It's okay you ate my muffin."

He laughs out loud and pulls out of the driveway. "Thank you. I really am sorry, but I couldn't help myself."

Tristan holds my hand in the car, linking his fingers with mine as I take bites out of my muffin.

"I thought we'd go to the pier," he says. "It's a nice place to sit for awhile."

"Sounds great," I say with my mouth full of muffin, and he grins and pulls into a parking lot. The air is already heavy and hot, but I like the heat on my skin. Tristan opens my door and takes my hand again, leading me down the pier. It's early enough so there are only a few other people about. Tristan walks me to the very edge and sits down, reaching his hand to me as I clamber down beside him. I copy him and take off my shoes so my toes can dip into the water. He kisses my forehead and I rest my cheek on his shoulder, swinging my feet.

I feel so much lighter than I did the night before, like I've released a part of some burden that's been plaguing me for so long. Tristan starts telling me a story about something Ethan said the other day and as I laugh I study his face. It's easy and open, so confident that it shakes me. But still humble. Still sweet enough to come over in the dead of night and then bring me half a blueberry muffin at dawn. I tilt my face up to his and feel his lips meet mine. I still am not sure I believe in this kind of thing happening at all, but I'm content for now to close my eyes in the warm morning sunshine and listen to the sound of his voice rise and fall like the waves beneath our feet.

CHAPTER 17
emma

The next week flies by with Tristan and me basically attached at the hip. He takes me surfing, which mostly entailed me lying on the beach while he surfed, and I take him on a walk around the cove near the inn. He's already charmed the pants off my mom, and it seems like she's gotten used to him running in and out of the house already. I didn't really think of making a formal introduction out of the whole thing; Tristan came in to grab me for a date and it just seemed natural for them to meet. She was trying to seem casual, but I know she's bursting with curiosity. Tristan and I have been together a lot, that much is true, but I'm still set on keeping things casual. The days before I leave are ticking down, even though going back to my job and San Diego seems less and less appealing with every day that passes. We're getting guests soon, too, and my days of endless freedom will be cut even shorter when I have to help my mom. For now, I'm enjoying my days in the sun, and Tristan. I've never had attention lavished on me this way, like he could sit next to me on the dock for hours just to listen to my voice. Our attraction isn't slowing down, either—it's intensifying. The thought concerns me the slightest bit, but I can handle it.

On another note, I'm getting more photography practice in lately than I have since high school. I take my camera everywhere that Tristan and I go. I glance over at the clock on my desk; Tristan is supposed to meet me in a few minutes. I'm standing in my room on one foot, leaning awkwardly out of my window in an effort to get the perfect aerial shot of my view. I'm so absorbed that I miss the sound of his wheels churning through the gravel, but I do hear his voice when he comes through the front door and greets my mom. His footsteps grow louder and louder and I shiver with anticipation, still aiming my camera through the window, trying to get off a couple more shots before he comes in and distracts me.

Tristan bursts through my door and wraps his arms around my waist from behind. I drop my camera on the bed, and my body is instantly tingling, as though my nerve endings are set off just by Tristan's touch. I smile as his mouth finds my neck, and try to control the waves of fire rolling through my limbs. I turn in his embrace and he kisses me, drawing me up against him and running his hands along my back. I press my body against him, feeling his chest against mine, his muscular stomach and thighs, all the places that have grown so familiar since we met. The ache returns between my legs as his mouth grows hotter and more insistent against mine, and a muffled moan escapes his throat. I pull away from him so we can both catch our breaths, and as he leans against me I can feel his hardness through his jeans. More and more, we've reached this point and stopped, and more and more I find myself wanting to do the opposite. He touches my cheek, and I lean into his touch.

"Hi," he says, grinning at me, his misty blue eyes lit up by the sun coming in through the window.

"Hi," I say back, leaning up on my tiptoes to kiss his jaw.

"Were you taking pictures?"

"Yup," I answer, grabbing my camera and turning it off. "Before you interrupted me."

"Sorry," he says, shrugging, and I know that he isn't. I smile at him, walking to a shelf by my bed to put my camera back in its case.

"You should bring it," he says.

"Now?"

"Yeah. There's good lighting out there right now. I think."

"Okay," I acquiesce, grabbing my camera and the case. I love that my camera is both automatic so I can snap as I go and that it's manual too, for when I want to set my own exposure and aperture. I've been playing around with Photoshop too, editing the photos I've taken so far, and I'm getting pretty good at using the tools. I already have plans for prints and I've been itching to get frames for a lot of them.

Tristan takes my hand and we walk down the stairs. My mom is sitting at the table in the dining room, going over some of the final touches for the downstairs bathrooms. She is filling more jars with sand and shells like she has in my room. She's even framed a few more of my photos. She looks up as Tristan and I come down the stairs, smiling at us.

"Where are you headed?" she asks, slipping her glasses off. "It's a beautiful day."

"We're going out on one of the boats," I say, practically bouncing up and down. Being out on the water with Tristan has quickly become my favorite activity. I can't believe it's been something I've missed out on until now. Tristan has even promised to help me learn to sail.

"I have the day off, so we're taking a day trip," says Tristan. "I'll have her back by tonight, Ms. LaVallie, if that's alright."

I resist the urge to roll my eyes, but my mom eats it up.

"That sounds fine," she says. "And thank you for helping me, Tristan. I think you were right about the blue."

"It was no trouble," says Tristan, smiling, and my mom shoos us out into the sunshine.

"What did you help her with?" I ask.

"She wants to put ribbon around the jars, or something. All I did was say which color I liked best."

He shrugs, and I wrap an arm around his waist as we make our way to the Jeep. He drapes an arm around my shoulders and kisses my head before reaching in to open my door for me. I balance my camera on my lap as we start toward the marina. Tristan parks and we make our way to the one he points out, tied up in the harbor. I bounce on board, already heading to the bow. I make sure the camera strap is around my neck—this thing is definitely not waterproof—and wait to fly out toward the horizon. I turn back to watch Tristan guide us out of the harbor.

"Is this what you want to do forever?" I ask, ducking under the rigging to join him at the wheel.

"What?"

"Sailing."

He glances at me, then refocuses on the water in front of us as he drives.

"Yeah," he says. "It's what I love."

I nod, studying his serious face.

Tristan angles the boat away from an incoming schooner and aims toward open water.

"But I want to do it a little differently than I am now," he says. "I've wanted to expand this business for a while. Incorporate more things than just driving people around the bay. I could teach sailing classes, water safety. I've always wanted to take a couple classes on boat construction, to learn more about it all."

"That sounds like a great idea."

"I'm not sure my dad will ever go for it. Someday, I'll get through to him, but not so far. I've got a big enough chunk in the business to do it anyway, but I don't want to, knowing the way he feels about it."

I nod, leaning into his shoulder. I know what it's like to have a dream that a parent doesn't approve of, and I like the fact that he's not just content to stay where he is for the next thirty years. He's happy, but he's looking for more, and I can identify with that.

Two hours later, I'm applying sunscreen for the second time and lying on a pink beach towel I've laid on the deck. The air is hot and still and so humid that little drops of sweat cover my skin and I've only been out of the water for a few minutes. A shadow covers me, and Tristan comes to lie next to me on the towel he's set up for himself, shaking the water out of his hair. The sun is starting to lower down into the sky, but it's far from night. I grope for my camera and snap a picture as Tristan lies down.

"I regret telling you to bring that thing," he says, and I giggle.

"No you don't," I say. "You like being my muse."

"It's true," he says, flipping onto his side like an Abercrombie model. I laugh, but it catches in my throat. Even though he's joking, he's pretty much perfect. Droplets of water run down his golden skin, catching in the definition of his muscles. I move over next to him and slide my arm around his waist. I lick the drops of water off his neck and I hear him groan. It gives me a quiet thrill to know that I make him feel this way, but lately we've also been riding a fine line between heaven and hell. Every time he's kissing me and it gets to be too much, we stop, but it's getting harder and harder to stay in control. Tristan snakes a hand around my hips and scoots me so close that we're pressed tight, and all that's separating us are a few insignificant scraps of material. He kisses my temple, my cheek, and then my mouth, caressing my face with his hand.

"Come to dinner tonight," he says, breaking his face away from mine.

"What?"

"My mom is making dinner. Enchiladas. I want you to come. If you want to."

It's such a simple request: enchiladas for dinner, just his family. Casual. But I recognize the offer as something more serious. Do I want to go down that road? Even as I hesitate, I look into his face and I know I can't say no to this man. He gives me so much without me ever having to ask, and even with the limitations of our relationship I find myself wanting to give something back to him.

"Of course," I answer, and he gives me a slow smile, the kind that makes me think I'm melting into a puddle as it unfolds across his face. My toes curl on my towel and I yank him toward me, kissing him hard and fast and desperately. I don't know how to control the emotion he brings out of me; with every day I spend with Tristan I feel more and more out of control and I'm losing the battle to keep it all in. What worries me is that I'm starting not to care.

CHAPTER 18

emma

A few hours later, we're docked again at the marina and Tristan is helping me off the boat. The sun is barely beginning to set over the water— my favorite time of the day.

I grab my camera and take a few shots. Tristan stands patiently next to me, and before he can protest I take a couple of his silhouette against the dying light. He just sighs, waiting for me to finish. I stuff my camera back into the case and we amble to the car.

"Are you ready for this?" he asks as we pull out of the parking lot, and for a second I'm worried he can see into my mind and knows that I feel a little torn about meeting his family. But with the grin on his face, I think he's teasing.

"I'm so ready," I answer, leaning back in my seat. "I'm starving." I start to play with the hem of my sundress and Tristan takes my hand, tracing circles on it with his thumb. I think he knows I'm a little nervous, but as I lean into his shoulder my anxiety evaporates. He pulls into a driveway in front of a little blue-gray house, and then follows the drive to a little cottage separate from the main property. The big house is situated just in front of this one, and there's a separate carport and everything for the bungalow. Tristan parks and comes around to open my door.

"Is this your parents' house?" I ask.

"Yeah. I live in the cottage."

"Got it," I say, swiveling my head around. "That's pretty convenient."

"It is," he says, leading me toward the house. "But lately I've started considering moving into my own place. You know, maybe put more than twenty feet between me and my parents."

"Why?"

"I'm not sure. I feel like a little extra space lately, for some reason. I should learn to cook for myself eventually, too, right?"

I laugh, and then we're at the door. Tristan takes my hands, pulling them away from the folds of my dress. I blush, knowing he's caught me twisting my hands in the fabric.

"Don't be nervous," he says. "I'll be right here with you the entire time."

How does he know that his presence is enough to calm me down?

I nod, and he kisses me quickly before opening the door.

"Mom! Dad? We're here."

The first one down the stairs is Ethan. He grins at Tristan and me as he takes the stairs two at a time.

"Hey, little brother," he says, slapping Tristan on the back.

"Did you move back in or something?" Tristan says to him.

"Nope. Here for dinner, just like you."

"What a coincidence," Tristan mutters.

His mom appears next, bustling in from the pantry; she's tiny, at least a foot shorter than her two sons, with dark hair piled in a bun on top of her head. She's wearing a flowered apron over her dress and I like her instantly.

"You must be Emma," she says, enveloping me in a hug. "We've heard so much about you." She releases me, beaming. "I'm Maggie, and this is Richard." Before I can answer, Tristan's dad sweeps in behind her and squeezes me into a bone-crushing hug that makes me gasp for breath.

"So good to have you," he says as he sets me back down, and I smile.

"It's nice to meet you both," I say, and my tension evaporates.

The enchiladas are delicious, and everyone is talking over each other as we eat. It's a medley of voices and laughter, but I don't feel left out. Tristan puts his hand on my leg every couple of minutes and Ethan passes me the rice without me asking for more. Tristan's mom scolds Tristan about something and they both laugh, and Ethan and his dad are including me in a conversation about San Diego. It's very comfortable, very homey, and I relax more and more as the night goes on. Before I know it, Maggie is asking me about my plans for the coming year.

"I'm not sure yet, honestly," I admit. "I'm thinking about college, but I could also keep working for another year or so."

"Emma is a photographer," says Tristan out of nowhere, and I immediately start to protest.

"Not really," I say, "it's just a hobby."

Tristan is already heading to the car to get my camera, and everyone else is asking me more about it. I do my best to answer everyone, worrying my hem to bits under the table. Tristan brings in my camera and turns it on so we can flip through the pictures on the little digital screen. There are pictures of the boat from today, of Tristan's face against the sky, the tide pools behind the inn. Richard stops on a photo of the boat we took out today that I snapped from the dock. Tristan's hands are the focus as he unties the ropes anchoring it to the gnarled wood.

"This is good stuff," says Richard. "Really good."

He flips through the next few pictures, all featuring parts of the boat while we were on the water. Ethan grabs the camera and starts looking through it.

"This is great," he says. "Emma, we could use something like these to promote Beyond the Sand."

"That's not a bad idea," says Richard.

"What?" All I can do is sit there while they flip through my photos.

"We've needed to get a website up forever," Tristan is saying.

"Can you take more like this?"

The question comes from Maggie, who looks me right in the eye. Everyone else stops their babbling and turns to me.

"Yeah, I could," I answer. That much is easy. "These photos haven't even been edited yet. I still have to crop them, adjust the lighting, the saturation."

"It's something to consider, Richard," Maggie says. "The photos are gorgeous, Emma."

"Thank you," I answer, beaming. No one has ever said that to me before, other than my mom. Then again, not many people have seen my photos other than her. They're hanging up all over my room at my dad's house but he doesn't pay much attention to them.

The conversation turns to other subjects again, and I'm relieved to have the bulk of the attention off of me. Even as the topic shifts, my mind is reeling with the possibility they presented me. To be able to be out on the water and snapping photos at the same time is second nature to me; to be able to do that and get paid to sell what I see is an absolute dream. Even to sell one picture at a time would be a start I could build from. I talk myself down in my head, but I know my face is flushed with color and Tristan takes my hand when he sees me fidgeting. He looks at me quizzically, and I smile and squeeze his hand to let him know I'm fine. He turns his attention back to the table and so do I, still wriggling with withheld excitement.

Dessert is served: New York style cheesecake with strawberries. I'm finishing up my second huge slice when I realize how much I love being surrounded by people like this. It's more than that—it's being surrounded by a family. I haven't been a part of something so whole in so long, haven't even realized how much I've been craving it. I miss my dad suddenly, and realize I need to call. I've been so busy that I've missed the times he's tried to reach me so far. I feel a stab of guilt. I'll try and remember tomorrow. Maggie asks about the bed and breakfast, and I'm quick to respond. I could talk about the inn all day; I feel like it's become as much my project as my mom's.

"We're expecting our first guests in the next few days," I say. "Everything is nearly ready. It's been a long process, but what my mom's done with everything, it's incredible."

"It really is," says Tristan. "You would never recognize it from what it was before."

"We would love to stay there sometime," says Maggie. "Just for fun. Your mom sounds wonderful."

"She is," I say, smiling. "And she'd love to have you."

Maggie beams and I realize I've just agreed that Tristan's parents should meet my mom. Is that going too far? I brush off the thought; I'm leaving too soon to have to worry about that. Not for the first time, a feeling of uneasiness makes my shoulders stiffen at the thought of leaving. It seems strange that not too long ago I was dreading coming here, and now I'm dreading the idea of going back. But I remind myself that I have to. I know that this, all of this, is temporary.

Finally, around nine thirty, Tristan's family relinquishes us. We're at the back door, everyone saying goodbye. Maggie hugs me one last time and Richard kisses my cheek in a fatherly way. I thank them one last time and then finally we are outside. Tristan walks me toward the Jeep, and we take one look at each other and start laughing.

"I thought we'd never get out of there," says Tristan, and I blow out a breath.

"Me, too," I say. We stop near the front door of the cottage, and I find myself studying it. It seems strange that Tristan has been in and out of my house so much since we've met, but I haven't even seen where he lives.

"Do you want to come in?" Tristan asks, reading my face perfectly, and I nod. He opens the door and leads me inside. It's so small, but cozy. The walls have rounded edges and the ceilings are vaulted so high it makes the rooms seem much bigger. He leads me through the living room and tiny kitchen upstairs to his bedroom. The bedframe is low to the ground and covered in dark blue sheets. The comforter is blue too, and lies neatly on top of the mattress. I notice the pillows are in place; Tristan is neat, much neater than me. I see his dresser and the closet and a TV set up across from the bed, and then the little desk and chair alongside it. Nothing is out of place. The downstairs is hardwood but his room is carpeted and fluffy under my toes.

"Well, here it is," he says, gesturing around. "There's not much to it."

"It's nice, though," I say, sitting down on the edge of his bed. "It's peaceful to have things so, I don't know, clean."

"Compared to your room it's military precise," says Tristan, laughing. He sits next to me, snagging my waist and pulling me to him. His lips meet mine and almost instantly my hands are fisted in his shirt and his are in my hair. We tumble backwards into the sheets, and he leans over me with his elbows on either side of my head. I wrap my arms around his neck and pull him closer until we're pressed together, his mouth hot on mine. I break away and kiss his jaw, his neck, as much as I can reach and I can feel his body hardening. His hands are on my face, his forearms pressed to the sides of my breasts, and he moves his mouth back to mine. His tongue slides into my mouth, and my body turns to liquid. My hands are reaching under his shirt to spread along his back, and finally I can't take it anymore and I push him off me and sit up.

He pauses, breathing heavily, and watches me as I stand up. I turn to face him, and as our eyes meet my breath catches in my throat. I don't stop to think. I reach behind me and unzip my dress until it pools onto the floor.

CHAPTER 19
tristan

All I can see is the glow of Emma's skin, bathed in light from the window. She steps out of the dress and all she's wearing is a bra and panties. Her hair is in a halo around her face, curls messy from lying on my bed, and her mermaid eyes are blazing into mine. She steps forward and climbs back onto my bed, and I'm so mesmerized I'm almost scared to touch her. I'm so hard I think I'm about to burst out of my jeans. Emma straddles me and I sit up; we're nose to nose and I am caressing her bare skin. She shudders as my hands skim from her hips to her shoulders and back again, her breasts pushed against my chest. Her bra is made of some silky material that slides against my skin, and her hands on my chest are making me crazy. I reach behind her and unsnap her bra and it slides off her shoulders, and I have never seen anything more fucking beautiful than Emma.

I kiss the hollow at the base of her throat, the skin over her heart, her collarbone, and then finally the creamy skin of her breast. Emma moans softly and leans her head back as I skim my lips, then my tongue, over her nipple. She writhes her hips in slow circles over mine as I shift to her other breast, cupping her ass in my hands. She is so perfect that I want to lavish attention on every inch of her but with her moving on me the way she is I don't think I can take that kind of time. She reaches behind me and pulls my shirt up and over my head and suddenly we're skin to skin for the first time.

I move her hair from her neck and run my tongue from her shoulder to her earlobe, biting it gently, and she digs her nails into my back. She jumps off me and pulls me to my feet and starts working at the button of my jeans. I don't fight her, don't even consider anything but letting her do exactly what she's doing. This scene is unfolding around me and focusing on anything except Emma is impossible. She pulls my jeans off and I kick them away and then she reaches for the band of my boxers. I shudder as she reaches in, exploring my skin, and then pulls them off, too. In the same moment I hook my thumbs into the waistband of her panties, tugging them off her hips. And then we're naked in front of each other and there's nowhere to hide, and I don't care.

I take her hand and pull her back onto the bed so she lands on her back with a thump. I climb on top of her, flattening myself against her and she moans as our skin connects, every inch of us. She reaches down, finds me and strokes in slow, smooth motions, and I grit my teeth. Her touch is almost too intense. I've tried this entire time to take things slowly, to keep things casual with Emma, but I can't. I'm so wrapped up in her that I can't hold anything back anymore. I kiss Emma's ribcage just below her breast, then skim my mouth down to her hips, then over her perfect legs. Her body is quivering as I spread her thighs with my hands, kissing the insides. Her skin is so soft, and so sensitive here that she shudders even though I'm barely touching her. I move higher.

"Tris . . ." she says as my mouth moves over her, and I think the sound of her saying my name is going to tear me apart. "Tris . . ."

She is smooth and wet and hot under my mouth, and as I take her hips in my hands I know I can't wait any longer. I reach over to my nightstand and pull a condom from the drawer, then tear open the foil and roll it over myself. Emma is panting, and I settle myself gently between her silky thighs. Before I can ask, she is already nodding.

"Yes," she says, "yes."

I lower myself down to her and slide inside, and the sensation is more than I can bear. I start to move and Emma wraps her legs around my waist and her hands dig into my hair. Her eyes are luminous, flooded with pleasure, and she leans up to nibble at my bottom lip as I move. I never knew it could be this way, that her body surrounding mine could be so completely overwhelming, but so intensely perfect at the same time. It's like a part of me I didn't know was missing clicks into place, and I'm whole. She whimpers as I start to move faster, and I pull her hands above her head and link her fingers with mine. Her eyes stare straight into mine, blurred as I take us higher and higher. Her fingers clench, and her body arches in rhythm with mine.

"Tristan . . . " she whispers, and her voice is my undoing. I bury my head in her neck, releasing her hands so I can wind them in her hair as I lose track of the world around me. There is only her.

CHAPTER 20
tristan

Maybe we sleep, or at least we kind of drift off. All I know is that I'm still on top of Emma when she sits up like a jack-in-a-box.

"Shit," she says, rolling off the bed and onto the floor, where she runs to her phone. "Shit," she says again, checking it. "My mom called like four times."

"What time is it?" I ask. "It can't be that late."

"It's midnight," says Emma, and we both stare dumbly at each other. Finally, I start laughing, and she giggles in response, covering her hand with her mouth.

"I could have sworn it was about nine fifteen and

that we just finished dinner," I say as I stand up and start yanking my pants on. "I'll take you home."

"Thanks," says Emma, and she steps in front of me, still naked. She wraps her arms around my neck and kisses me softly, tenderly. I stroke her hipbones with my hands and kiss her back, pouring everything I can't say into this moment. There is an aching in my chest, a physical pain as I bite back the words I want to say, knowing she doesn't want to hear them.

Emma pulls back and gazes into my eyes, lifting a hand to my face, and I see an expression I've never seen before in her eyes. Then a shutter flicks down and she turns away, grabbing her clothes, but I saw it, and it makes me hope. I reach for her zipper and pull it up without her having to ask me, and she rewards me with a smile.

The car ride to Emma's feels like a dream, one I don't want to end. She draws circles with her thumb over my hand as we drive, her head on my shoulder.

"I wish you didn't have to go," I say.

"Me, too," she sighs. "My mom is going to be mad. I'll tell her we fell asleep."

"That's not a total lie," I say, and Emma laughs.

"True. We must have slept for at least a little while."

We pull into her driveway, and Emma releases my hand and turns to me. I look into her perfect face and I find myself wanting so badly to tell her how I feel. Maybe, I think, as she looks at me. Maybe now she's ready to be honest with herself about her feelings. Maybe she's ready to hear it. But as I open my mouth, she beats me to it.

"I had a really great time tonight," she says. "But I want to make sure we're both remembering that I'm leaving soon, and where this whole thing is going."

Every warm feeling I had from tonight drops into coldness. Why did she have to say that to me right now, like I'm a child that needs to be reminded of the rules? Is she really so cold that she has to tell me I better not fall in love with her, because she won't feel the same? I thought we had a chance of moving past this point, but I guess I was wrong. And I'm not only one who has to deal with this, it's her, too. Because I know what's happening here, and I know it isn't only happening to me. She is feeling things she doesn't want to and she's trying to back off. Well, it's not going to work. I know that, even if she doesn't. It still hurts to hear her say that to me. Especially after tonight.

"I know," is all I say. "I remember the rules, Emma."

I spit out the last sentence with more venom than I mean to, and she frowns. I compose my face and stare back at her evenly. I can't let her know how much she gets to me and how badly I want her to change her mind.

"Okay, then," she says, and leans in hesitantly to kiss me goodbye. I brush my lips over hers and then get out of the car and open her door, avoiding touching her. She has a wrinkle of concern between her brows, which normally I would think was cute, but not now. I have to pull myself back the way she has, and close myself off so I don't end up being the idiot that gets hurt. Deep down I know it's not going to work, but I don't know what else to do. I have to keep trying to change her mind, and hope she'll see the truth before it's time for her to go.

"'Bye," she whispers, kissing my cheek, and I manage to give her a small smile.

"'Bye, Emma," I say, watching her walk to the door. She steps onto the porch and gives me a little wave before going inside, and I wave back. As soon as her front door shuts I jump into the Jeep and take off. What the hell am I supposed to do with this girl? How am I supposed to act like this is a summer fling when I'm already halfway in love with her?

CHAPTER 21
tristan

That night is a restless one; I keep reaching to the other side of the bed, searching for Emma. Her scent lingers on my pillow and on my skin, and it makes even my own space distracting. I finally sit up around five and give up trying to sleep. I turn on the shower and stand under the hot spray, letting it clean my skin of her touch. Dammit, why did she have to remind me that this is supposed to be casual? And why last night? I lean my head on the tiled wall, letting the water pour over me. I don't know what I'm supposed to do. I grab the shampoo and then the soap, washing myself clean, and then shut the water off. After I pull on sweats and a T-shirt I walk to my parents' house, hoping for food. My mom is already in the kitchen in her peppermint-striped bathrobe, pulling cinnamon rolls out of the oven.

"Morning, Ma," I say, reaching for a lick of the icing she's about to drizzle on top, and she slaps my hand away like I knew she would.

"Wait until they've cooled a little, Tristan," she scolds. "Or I'll kick you out of my kitchen."

I lean against the kitchen counter, waiting as she spreads icing over the rolls.

"Your father and I liked Emma," she says with her back to me. Hearing her name brings a bittersweet jolt—happiness mixed with frustration.

"That's good," is my only response, and my mom turns to me.

"Did you feel strange having her here?"

"No, not at all." I run a hand through my hair and over my face. "I loved having her here with you guys."

"What's wrong? Did she not like us?"

I burst out laughing at my mom's horrified expression.

"No, Ma, she loved you. It's not that."

"Well, then, what's the issue?"

It's never been typical of me to open up about this kind of stuff, especially with my mom, but Emma is a different case simply because she's, well, different.

"I don't think she likes me the same way I like her."

"Why would you think that, Tris?" My mom puts a roll on a plate and hands it to me, and I dig in, still leaning against the counter.

"She's just always reminding me that she's leaving soon, heading back to California. And she always says she wants our relationship to be casual, but it's not easy."

"It sounds like she's afraid. Because I saw the way she was with you, and there was nothing casual about it."

"I don't know how to make her see that. We're great together, and I really care about her. I don't want to marry her or anything, but she runs away even from the idea of us being serious."

"Well, think practically here, Tristan. How would

you be together? Are you going to move to San Diego? Is she going to move here? Do you want to live 3,000 miles from the person you're dating?"

My mom makes a good point, the way she always does, but this one hits home harder than usual.

"I don't know," I answer honestly. "My life is here. Hers could be, too, I think, if she wanted it to be."

"Speaking of which," says my mom, "if you are going to talk to Emma today, let her know we're definitely interested in buying several of those photos from her. Your father and I talked about it last night."

"Seriously? Wow, Ma . . . that's great." I know how completely excited Emma will be about this, and I can't wait to tell her. It might only be a few of her photos, but that's better than nothing.

"One more thing, Tris," says my mom. "I can see you care about this girl, and that's great. I'm happy to see you with someone who makes you so happy. But don't go giving yourself to someone who won't be there for you the way you would be for her."

All I can do is stare. I understand what my mom

is saying, and it hurts to have Emma refer to our relationship as impermanent, but she also makes it so hard to pull anything back from her. Regardless of how she feels, I know I have to keep trying to make her see how much I care, and that this relationship is worth fighting for. I can't let her leave thinking that I was just a summer fling. So all I do is nod at my mom and then dart out the door to prepare for a tour I'm leading later. I don't know how all this is going to work. I don't know if it's possible. I picture Emma as she pulled her dress over her head and a part of me knows she's worth everything.

After my afternoon tour, which was a big group of tourists from North Dakota, I am more convinced than ever that my Beyond the Sand's services could be expanded. I could hold sailing camps for kids and even provide photography tours for people like Emma who would be interested in the chance to take pictures they could print and frame after their vacation. I escort my group back to the parking lot, thanking everyone for coming. My phone vibrates and it's a text from Emma, reminding me that this is her last night before the first guests arrive. We're supposed to do something together since her time will be more limited after today. It also reminds me that she's supposed to be leaving in a few weeks. Despite everything that's happened, I can't wait to see her. It feels like an eternity since I've held her. I shake my head at myself. Even with everything going on and how complicated she's making my life, at the end of the day I care about her a lot. I think I'd do anything to make her happy. There's a lingering doubt hidden in my mind, though, that she would do the same for me.

CHAPTER 22

tristan

I head for Emma's at seven thirty, even more excited than usual. I spent the rest of the afternoon signing up for a few classes at the community college in Newport. I'm going to start a beginning engineering class and a course in marketing to help out with the new sector of business I'm hoping to start. I also get to tell Emma that she's about to sell her first pictures to my parents, a few to use for the new website we're going to make. I pull into Emma's drive and turn off my Jeep. As I open the door, the front door of the house opens and she's standing there in a red sundress and sandals. Her toes are painted bright pink. As always, I forget everything but how gorgeous she is.

"Tristan!" she says, running to grab my hand. She kisses me twice, hard and fast, and then drags me inside.

"I want you to see everything," she says. "It's all ready, all perfect for when the guests get here."

Inside, everything is immaculate. Emma and her mom have gone completely all-out; every surface is shining or swept clean, and there are decorations everywhere. It's beautiful but welcoming, like you're a member of the family, coming for a visit. Emma and her mom walk me through every room and each one looks better than the one before. When we wind up at the front door, Emma is beaming, and her mom looks happy too, but tired.

"Have a good time tonight," she says to Emma, giving her a hug. She smiles up at me, too. I can see Emma's eyes resemble hers, although Emma's are more blue and her mom's lean toward green.

"Thank you, Ms. LaVallie," I say. "I'll have her back soon."

Then there's nothing but Emma's hand in mine and her voice in my ear, and I feel like that's all I'll ever need.

We walk down to the little cove below the inn, where I first saw Emma. It's low tide, and the tide pools are filled with anemones, urchins, and sea stars. Once we are out of sight of the inn the beach is completely private. I hold Emma's hand and we explore as she points out every little creature she finds. I listen, mostly, enjoying being in her presence.

"I'm so excited for the guests to arrive," she says. "But I'm nervous. We've been preparing for so long it was starting to feel like it would be my mom and me forever."

"The inn looks ready," I say honestly. "You've done an amazing job."

"Thanks," she says. "It was my mom, mostly. She believed in that place when no one else did."

"Did you live there as a kid?"

"No," she answers as her eyes cloud. "She started fixing it up after her and my dad split up."

"Was that hard for you?"

Emma stalls, tucking her hair behind her ear, the sunset shining behind her. Waves wash up to our feet over and over, and I wait for her to open up to me.

"Yes," she says, "it was. I wish it had all been easier."

"How old were you?"

"I was in junior high."

"And your dad ended up with full custody?"

"Yes," says Emma quietly, wrapping her arms around herself. "My mom didn't even fight for me."

"What do you mean?"

"In court. She stood there, didn't cry once, or yell. She just stood there."

"Is that how your dad got full custody?"

"He testified that she had a drinking problem," Emma whispers, the words pouring out like sand in an hourglass. "He said she couldn't provide the safe home environment I needed." Her voice is bitter and harsh.

"Your mom is an alcoholic?"

Emma turns her tortured gaze to me. "I don't have any memories of her drinking," she says. "None at all."

"That seems weird."

"It was. The whole thing was completely surreal. But she still didn't argue, she just stood there, silent."

"Maybe she was trying to protect you somehow," I say. "That's what it sounds like to me."

Emma shrugs, and as her shoulders fall it becomes infinitely clearer to me why her views on love are so jaded. She's an only child, and there was no one to share the burden of grief. The two parents took their anger out on each other, and Emma got the whiplash.

"Your mom loves you, Emma," I say. "That much is obvious. Maybe a part of her was afraid, too, that what they were saying was true. Maybe she was afraid she wouldn't be able to give you the life she wanted to, and that you would be better off with your dad."

Emma stares out over the water, and I'm sorry to be talking about something that upsets her. I want her to understand that she can tell me how she feels, that I am here for her.

"I guess," is all she says, and I let it go.

"I have something to tell you," I say, taking her hand. She turns to me as a breeze blowing over the ocean catches her hair.

"What is it?"

"My parents want to buy a few of your photos for sure. My mom told me this morning."

"Are you serious?" A smile is breaking over her face like sunshine, and we're both laughing for no reason.

"Yeah, totally serious. They're gonna buy them, Emma."

"Oh my God."

She covers her mouth with her hands, laughing, and then leaps into my arms.

"That's amazing," she breathes into my ear, her arms around my neck. I bury my face in her hair and breathe her in. After last night, everything with her feels more intimate, more personal. Whether Emma likes it or not, we know each other on a different level now. I know she feels it as she pulls back to look at my face. She traces my jaw, tilting her head and studying me like never before.

"What?" I ask.

She shakes her head silently. "Nothing," she whispers.

An electric shock passes between us as our lips connect. I'm surrounded by her, her scent and her body and everything else, and it completely throws me. I'm so in love with this girl. She can't go. I can't let her go. I lower Emma to her feet and lay my sweatshirt on the sand, then tug her down with me. She lies back, and I swear I can see her heart shining out of her eyes. I wish she could say it, I wish I could say *it*, but I try to be content with showing it, pushing away this ache in my chest. I tangle my hands in her hair, kissing her temples and her nose. She smiles, caressing my back, and tilts her face up to mine. Her lips are soft, teasing, then hot as her mouth opens. She pushes against my chest and rolls us over so she is leaning over me. The fading light shimmers behind her, making her look like she's glowing.

"I remember the first time I saw you," I say. "Standing on this beach. I thought you were pretty then, but now you're the most beautiful thing I've ever seen."

Emma pauses, staring at me. A strap of her dress has fallen off her shoulder and her hair is a wild mess of red and gold.

"Tristan," she whispers.

Her voice is low and tender. She leans down, her breasts pressing against my chest. She kisses me hard, fiercely, and it grows so intense that stopping isn't an option. I let her tug my shirt over my head, and she runs her hands over me, her mouth fused to mine. I work at the zipper of her dress and she lets her arms out of the straps. It folds down her front and then her breasts are in my hands, in my mouth. I'm painfully hard, straining in my jeans. I'm trying to be patient and take things slowly, but Emma makes it nearly impossible. She climbs onto my lap, arching her back to press her breasts into my mouth. I use my tongue on her nipples until she cries out. I reach underneath her dress for the heat between her legs, and she whimpers in my ear.

"Tristan," she says. "Tristan, now."

"Hold on, just hold on," I pant as I try to move, but she puts a hand on my chest.

"Do you have something?" she asks, and I grab the condom from my jeans pocket. Emma gives me enough space to yank my jeans and boxers down and I hand her the condom. She opens it and rolls it down me, inch by inch, and I nearly lose control. Emma raises herself up and guides me into her until we're connected. I grip her hips, trying to be gentle but knowing my fingers will leave marks on her skin. She leans down so her breasts brush my chest and tangles her fingers in my hair as she moves. I pull her mouth to mine. Her breath rushes out faster and faster and my hips move against her in a rhythm neither of us can control. As she collapses on top of me I hold her as tightly to me as I can, like if I can get her close enough we might never have to say goodbye.

I walk her back to the inn as it gets dark. Our hands are linked and we're walking as slowly as possible, putting off saying goodnight for as long as we can. Emma has been pretty quiet, and I have, too. I'm feeling so much that it's hard to put into words, and what's worse is I'm worried she won't want to hear it. I want to tell her that I don't want her to go, but the words stick in my throat, maybe out of habit. I've gotten used to it over the past weeks.

"Look at the stars," says Emma, turning to point up at the sky. It looks like millions and millions of pulsing lights against the black background. I come up behind Emma and link my arms around her waist, and she leans back into my embrace.

"I don't want this night to end," she whispers, and I kiss the side of her neck.

"Me, either."

"I'll be busier now, with the bed and breakfast, but I can still see you. We'll just have to plan around our schedules."

I nod against her hair, glad to hear her talking about the future, even if it's only in the short term.

"I can't believe I'm leaving so soon," she says, and her words make me go cold.

"I know," I say.

"It seems so fast."

"Why don't you stay longer?" It's out before I can take it back. Emma shifts in my arms.

"Like, stay another few days?"

"Yeah. Or, you know, you could just not leave." There it is. I said it.

"I have to leave, Tristan."

"You don't, though. Not really. You're not even sure what you want to do next year."

She turns around to face me and folds her arms.

"Yeah, exactly. I need to figure that out before I think about moving across the country."

"Give it some thought, Emma. That's all I'm saying." I ease off, letting her have space to think. Her shoulders relax a little and she takes my hand again.

"I will," she says softly, and we continue toward the inn. We stop at the front door and I take her in my arms, kissing her softly. I wish I could hold her all night. The thought of going home to my own bed sounds lonely and cold.

"Good luck tomorrow," I say, kissing her cheek. "You're going to be great."

"Thanks, Tris," she says, smiling at me. "I'll miss you."

For Emma, that's pretty fucking romantic.

"I'll miss you too, baby," I say, and she kisses me harder, her hands in my hair. "Sweet dreams."

"Goodnight," she says, and then she turns and slips inside the big front door, closing it gently behind her. I stuff my hands in my pockets and walk to the car, my mind still full of her. She said she's going to miss me. I hope she just meant tomorrow and not for the rest of her life.

CHAPTER 24

tristan

The next few weeks race by even quicker than the ones before it.

Emma's first day at the inn goes amazingly well. The constant rotation of guests keeps her and her mom busy. There's laundry to deal with, and cooking for everyone, and a million things to take care of. In Emma's spare time, and mine, we're always together. It gets to be so much of a pattern that I just make my way to her house at the end of my day, or call her as soon as I finish a tour. Our parents start expecting us to be together. I came home without Emma the other day and my mom almost had a heart attack.

But underneath the happiness of every minute I spend with Emma is the realization that time is slipping between my fingers. I never thought about the concept of time so much in my life until Emma. Now it preoccupies my mind every hour of the day, and the more I try to hold onto it, the faster it seems to go.

Emma is leaving in a couple of days and I still don't know how to get her to stay.

It's hard to believe I've only known her for such a short period of time when it feels as though I've known her all my life. I feel like I was floating when I met her, content with where I was but stuck in the same place. I'm ready to move forward now, to do something more. But I don't want to do it without Emma.

I'm sitting in my room after a shower looking for apartment listings on my laptop when I get her text. It's just a normal night, and I've been waiting for her response so I know when to come pick her up. We have plans to see a movie, and maybe take a walk on the beach afterward. I'm already impatient to see her, and I grab my phone. I open her text.

I need you to come over here. Now.

That doesn't sound good.

CHAPTER 25

emma

I'm pacing my room over and over again; it feels like a prison. I count the days on my hand again, just to be sure. Three days. It's been three days too long. I run my hands through my hair, fighting back tears. Where is Tristan? It's already been such a long day, and now this. Finally, I see his headlights and I wait another agonizing minute for him to make it up to my room. I pull him in and shut the door behind him. He is already at my side, his face a mask of concern.

"Emma," he says, "what's wrong?" He takes my face in his hands. Just his presence calms me, but I'm still so scared.

"I'm late," I whisper, and his jaw tightens.

"What do you mean?"

"My period, Tristan. My period is late."

"By how long?"

"Three days."

"That's not that much time."

"I always start on the same day," I say as tears flood my eyes again. "Always. And it's been three days too long."

"Did you just realize today?"

"Yes. A guest asked for tampons and it made me think about it."

"Emma, it's probably fine. We've used condoms."

"They're not 100% effective, Tristan."

We stand there staring at each other, two people scared to death by the same situation. I can tell Tristan is as worried as I am, although he hides it better than me. He runs a hand over his head and then down his face. I can't stand it; I walk straight into his arms. He rubs my back and I breathe him in, letting him calm me. His chest is warm and familiar, but his heartbeat in my ears is too fast.

This can't be happening, but it is happening, and I have to handle it.

"I need a pregnancy test," I say. "A good one, one of the sensitive ones. Can they tell this early?"

"I'm not sure, but I think so. I can go get one now."

"Okay. Hurry, please."

"I will. Emma, it'll be fine."

He kisses me once, hard, and then bolts back out the door. Luckily, everyone is tucked in for the night. It's been a crazy day. We have guests in every room, and checking them in and getting everyone situated has taken forever. My mom is so good at this kind of stuff; she directs me and I do exactly what she says. We're really starting to find a pattern, the pair of us. The first day was such a mess—I was, at least—she was perfectly composed. But now I've adjusted to the rhythm of running the inn, and I'm actually pretty comfortable with it. And I enjoy it much more than I thought I would: meeting the guests, helping them get settled, giving them tips about the area as though I belong here.

Everything has been running smoothly, though, until today, when I realized I was late.

I stop in my tracks.

How many days has it been? I do the math again in my head, but I've done it enough to know I'm counting right. If I'm pregnant I don't know what I'm going to do. I look down at my flat tummy and try to calm my breathing. I'm leaving in four days. I can't be pregnant; Tristan and I aren't even together, not really. I shove down the little voice in my head that's been growing increasingly stronger lately that says I am. But I'm not. I don't love him and we're not together and I cannot be pregnant because I can't do this. I sit down on the edge of my bed, my fear suddenly outweighed by anger. Didn't I learn long ago that love was a dangerous thing, and not to be trusted? And there I went, anyway, even though I knew better. I'm an idiot, thinking I could come so close to love and not get burned somehow.

CHAPTER 26
emma

The tears are flowing again as Tristan's lights flood the driveway. I fervently pray that my mom is in her room or the kitchen or something and doesn't see Tristan walk in with a box of pregnancy tests. I hear his footsteps on the stairs and then he's in my room with the plastic bag.

"I got three different kinds," he says, pulling out boxes. "This one says it can detect pregnancy before you've even missed your period, so I think it should be able to tell."

"Give me that one," I say, and he passes me a box and I stride straight into my bathroom and shut the door. I rip open the box so hard that little white tests fly out in every direction; I grab one off the floor and sit down on the toilet. When I finish, I read the directions: "Wait sixty seconds for results." I set the test on the sink counter and count to sixty in my head. I can't breathe with my chest in knots like this. One of my cuticles starts to bleed as I gnaw at the nail, waiting. I wish Tristan was in here with me, and the thought frightens me nearly as much as the possibility of being pregnant. I sit alone, instead, tapping my foot on the cold tile and fighting the shudders in my chest that comes with a new batch of tears in my eyes. Sixty seconds has never taken so long.

When the count is finished I pick up the test. My hands shake so badly I almost drop it. I look down at the little box. There is one pink line. Which line am I looking at? The control line or the other one? I grab the box and read the directions again. They say clearly that two lines is pregnant, and one is not. Not pregnant.

I'm not pregnant.

"Are you okay in there?" Tristan says into the back of the door, and I open it.

"Hand me another box," I say, and he does without asking why.

I try another test, this one with words instead of lines. The words "Not Pregnant" pop up in the little square. I breathe another sigh of relief. The knots in my chest unravel ever so slightly. But why is my period late? I think I remember reading somewhere that a girl's period can be affected by things like stress. Maybe that's all this is: stress. I open the bathroom door and Tristan is standing there with his hands in his pockets.

"I'm not pregnant," I say.

He braces his hands on his knees. "Oh, thank God," he breathes. Then he wraps me in his arms.

"Damn, you scared me. When I walked in here you looked like a corpse."

"I'm sorry. I was freaking out."

"I was too, for a minute. I was worried I was going to have to marry you and take care of a baby." He shakes his head wryly, sitting on the edge of my bed.

"Be serious," I say, joining him. "You wouldn't marry me. I wouldn't let you if you tried."

"Why do you say that?" He looks at me quizzically, and I laugh in disbelief.

"Tristan, be serious. I would take care of it."

"What do you mean, take care of it?" His voice is lower and somehow colder, catching me off guard.

"I would probably have an abortion, Tristan. I'm barely nineteen. I'm not ready for a baby."

"Well neither am I, but I would take care of you if it happened. I would handle my responsibility."

I roll my eyes. "I don't need you to take care of me, or handle anything. And I would never marry you."

A look of pain crosses his face, and I want to swallow my words.

"I just mean, I don't think I'd marry anyone," I try to explain. "I don't really believe in it anymore. And I wouldn't marry you only because I was pregnant."

"You're never going to let me in, are you?" says Tristan.

He stands up off the bed and looks at me.

I gape at him. I've never seen him look so distant from me. With a shock of realization, I wonder if this is how I look to him when I shut down.

"Tristan—" I start, but he walks away from me, facing the window. I don't know what to say. "For God's sake," I protest. "I'm not pregnant. It's not even an issue."

"But if it was, you would go and get an abortion and take care of it without even asking me. It's not the abortion itself that bothers me, it's that you wouldn't even consider something as simple as letting me be there for you. That's how you are, Emma. You keep everything in and push everyone away."

"I'm not even pregnant! I don't know what you're angry about."

He shakes his head, staring outside. "Do you know how I feel about you, Emma?"

"What? I mean, yeah. You like me the same way I like you."

I have a feeling this is going to go somewhere I don't want it to, but I'm powerless to stop it. My hands are cold, like my fingertips have turned to ice even as I turn them in my lap over and over.

"You know that's not what I mean."

"Tristan, don't do this. Please."

"Don't what? Don't be honest with you?"

"Just don't go there. It won't change anything."

"Oh, that's good. Good to know that saying I love you won't change a damn thing."

I bow my head, bringing my hands up to cover my face. I knew, of course I knew. But I didn't want to. It makes everything so much harder.

"I can't do this, Emma," says Tristan, and my head snaps up. He is facing me now, his eyes dark and sad.

"Do what?"

"I can't be with you and not tell you how I feel. I can't let you go back to California like you don't mean anything to me."

"You knew what this was, Tristan. You know I don't feel the same way about you."

"Yes, you do."

My entire body goes numb. He is staring into my eyes and I'm hypnotized, paralyzed by his words. Of course he knows. I'm transparent to him. I have been since day one. But I didn't know he'd be able to see something I haven't admitted even to myself.

"No," is all I say, but my voice quivers and I know he knows I'm a liar.

"You do," he says quietly. "And I can't live like this. I'd rather not be with you than keep acting like this is some casual fling, that neither of us cares about the other, that it's totally fine if you get an abortion without considering how I feel."

Tears are flowing down my face, and I notice his eyes are glassy.

"It's not fair of you to ask that of me, Emma. You want me when you need me, like tonight, and you push me away when you don't. You make me hold everything back from you because you're so damn scared of love. And you knew, you knew it was hurting me, and you did it anyway."

"I never meant to hurt you," I whisper. "Never."

"But you knew. You knew and you were too scared to admit the truth to either of us."

It's too much for me to hear, but I know every word is right. In trying to keep myself safe, I have hurt him. And he never deserved that. I want to go to him and let him take all the pain away, to run to him and say that he's right. But I can't.

"I don't know what you want me to do," I answer.

"I want you to stop lying to yourself. And I want you to admit that our love is important and significant enough for you to actually consider it love, and consider letting it change your life a little. You're so damn stubborn, Emma. You would rather be hurt by something you're hiding from than accept the truth."

"Life isn't a fairy tale, Tristan," I say. "Love ends, and people hurt each other. I was only trying to protect both of us."

"And how did that work out, Emma? Pretty well?"

He's never spoken to me like this, with so much pain and disgust in every word. Each syllable is another stinging blow. I'm reeling from this conversation, and all my safe places have been exposed. There's nowhere to hide, nowhere to run.

"I think you should go," I say, but Tristan is already walking away, leaving my bedroom door cracked open as he goes. Even in his anger, he is too much of a gentleman to slam the door. I sit on my bed like a statue as tears flood down my cheeks. There is that ache in my chest again, and I rub it with my palm. I went from doing everything in my power not to get hurt to hurting more than I've ever known. I curl up in a ball. He was right, too. He was right about everything.

CHAPTER 27
emma

Some time later, my mom knocks on my door. "Emma? Emma, are you alright?"

I don't answer, and she opens the door and sees me lying on the bed.

"Emma, what in the world?"

My mom comes and sits next to me and I start sobbing. The whole story comes out, and my mom just listens quietly, stroking my hair. Finally I stop, my throat raw from talking and crying.

"I messed up," I whisper. "I feel like an idiot."

"Emma, it's going to be alright."

I can feel the words bubbling up inside me, and I can't lock them down anymore.

"Why didn't you fight for me, Mom?"

My mom stiffens next to me and looks down into my eyes. "What in the world are you talking about?"

"The divorce. You didn't cry in court, you didn't plead. You let the lawyers walk all over you and you didn't even defend yourself." It's the question I've always wanted to ask, but never had the courage to.

"Oh, Emma, I wish I had an easy answer. It's so complicated. The lawyers . . . and your father, he . . . " My mom shakes her head. "But of course I wanted you, Emma."

She stands up, wrapping her arms around herself.

"What about the drinking?" I ask quietly. "I remember that part so clearly."

Her shoulders draw back, as though she's bracing herself for a fight.

"I was never a drinker. You know that. I don't have the stomach for it. But when your father and I started fighting, I would go into the kitchen and pour myself a drink. It became a habit, and your father hated it. He used it against me, exaggerating the details. I haven't had a drop since that trial ended." She turns back to me, coming to the bed and taking my hands.

"You could have denied it, though," I say. "You could have argued."

"Emma, I tried. My lawyers advised me to. I tried to open my mouth a thousand times but every single time the only thing I saw was your face. You were so sad back then, Emma. Sadness radiated from your entire body. You were so quiet during that time, so hard to reach. I couldn't bring myself to cause more grief between your father and I, to make even more of a scene. I wanted to make things better for you."

I'm holding her hands so tightly I'm afraid I'm hurting her, but she just rubs her thumbs over my knuckles.

"And even more than that, I had started to believe them. Your father, his lawyers, they painted this picture of a mother unfit to take care of you. I had spent so long fighting with your father that I didn't believe in anything anymore, including myself. I was afraid they were right, afraid you really would be better off away from me. I might not have done it in the right way, but I was so lost at that time. I'm sorry for that, Emma. I'm sorry for everything we put you through."

I don't know how to process what's happening. For most of my life I've held my mother's abandonment on my heart like a scar, and now, that entire perception has shifted. I still love my dad, I always will, but I love my mother for the sacrifice she thought she had to make to save me. I can't believe it's been so long and I'm just now finding this out. A weight lifts from my chest that I didn't know was there, but I'm still in the middle of a mess. I reach for my mom and hug her, letting that say more than words ever could. She sighs into my hair, and I hope she feels better now that I know. I let her go and sink back to the bed.

"I don't know what to do," I whisper. "About anything."

"In terms of Tristan, that's up to you, Emma. But if you do love him, you can't pretend you don't. That's how both of you ended up hurt. It's not fair for you to ask him to be with you but to hold back at the same time."

I nod, playing with the quilt on my bed. "I'm not sure it's what I want."

My mom nods, rubbing circles on my back.

"In terms of next year, you're more than welcome to live with me. You could apply to college here."

"I really want to go," I whisper. "I want to study what *I* want to study, and not what someone else thinks I should."

"I know. Consider it, Emma. You can be anything you want. Whatever you decide—San Diego, here, with your father . . . you know I'll be here."

She pulls me into a hug and I cry for the thousandth time that night. All of a sudden, everything's changed, and I don't know what I'm going to do about it. I let my mom hold me and I close my eyes, hoping that in the morning, things will be clearer.

CHAPTER 28

emma

I wake up with gritty eyes and a heavy heart. My phone shows no missed calls or texts from Tristan, and when I get up to use the bathroom in the morning, I find my period has started. I shake my head; maybe if I hadn't been so worried, we never would have had this fight. A bigger part of me knows that it would have happened either way; it was inevitable. I knew how he was feeling, and how I was feeling, I just didn't want to admit it. But now, just like that, everything is different. I'm not the same girl I was yesterday. I need to make things right, if I can, and I need to call my dad and talk about next year. I'm still planning on going back to San Diego in a few days, but it might be to pack my things. I change out of my pajamas and head outside. My mom said she could handle things at the inn for a bit while I sort everything out. I blink in the sunlight and sigh. I've made a huge mess of things, but hopefully I can make them right again.

CHAPTER 29

tristan

I haven't slept all night. Whenever I close my eyes I see her smile, hear her laugh, and I know I'll most likely never see her again. Why did I have to go and say all those things to her? I did exactly what she didn't want, and look how it worked out. But I couldn't help it. I couldn't go another day living the same lie and acting like the way I loved her wasn't changing me, because it is, and it has. The sting of knowing I've lost her hurts even worse than I imagined. I'm sitting on my bed, wondering how I'm going to summon the energy to direct a tour I'm scheduled for at ten, when I hear her voice.

"Tristan? Are you there?"

My front door opens, and I hear footsteps. I'm frozen just knowing she's near. She walks into my room, and my heartbeat doubles in speed the way it does every damn time I see her. She's wearing jean shorts and a tank top and her hair is in a ponytail and she looks as tired as I feel. The realization gives me hope.

"What do you want?" I ask, and she locks her hands together. She looks more vulnerable than I've ever seen her; the mask that usually hides her emotions has fallen. Her eyes are wide and clear and she looks hesitant, sincere.

"I want to apologize," she says, and my heart thunders even harder. But the sting of last night is still fresh, and I'm still conditioned to hide my feelings around her. That's not something I'm sure I'll ever get over.

"I did everything wrong," she says. "I shouldn't have tried to hide my feelings and I shouldn't have made you hide yours. I just thought . . . I thought love was something to be avoided at all costs. You've heard a little about how things were with my parents.

I finally resolved some of that last night, but it's still going to take me awhile to learn to completely trust somebody. You're the only person who has ever made me want to do that."

Her eyes have dark circles underneath them, and her voice is raspy, but her gaze is calm and direct.

"You made me feel things that I thought I needed to hide. I thought it would make things safer, and easier on both of us in the long run. I didn't expect to love you so easily, or so quickly."

To hear her admit it is a balm to my wounds, but I'm still in pain.

"I'm still not sure what's going to happen, but I couldn't not tell you this," she continues. "I owe you that much."

"You don't owe me anything," I say, and her smile fades. "Look, Emma," I start. "I appreciate you coming here and saying all this. Really, I do. But there's been too much damage."

Emma looks so fragile and sad that I want to go to her and take her in my arms, but I can't. I'm still hurting from the way things turned out; the pain is too fresh.

"I don't think I can fix it," I say. "I loved you, and I still think I do, but hiding it was . . . it was awful. I don't know if I can undo the way I felt when I was holding everything back for your sake. I think I'm about all out of tries."

There is a brief pause where the only sound is my breathing and hers. She is still standing there, and it hurts to look at her. All of the bullshit aside, I love her. But right now my mind is clouded with confusion. And I'm angry—there's no denying that. It's been building up throughout the summer just like all the words I wanted to say but couldn't.

"That's okay," she says quietly. "I understand. Um, I'll just go. I'm gonna go."

She comes forward suddenly and kisses my cheek.

"I'm so sorry," she says. "Goodbye, Tristan."

She turns and walks away from me, leaving nothing behind but her scent and this awful feeling that I'm losing something I'm never going to get back. The silence is deeper somehow now that she's been here and then left again, and it makes my chest ache. I shake it off and stand up, ready to go do my tour. I bury the pain and set out to my Jeep, determined to forget about her.

CHAPTER 30
tristan

Hour by hour, I feel worse instead of better. I finish my tours for the day and drive home again, going right to bed even though it's still early. I toss and turn all night, unable to get comfortable. Emma's words ring in my mind, over and over. I see her eyes, honest and afraid, and I watch them fill with tears again and again as my mind replays the moment. Finally around five in the morning I shower and try to read, but nothing feels right. Everything feels foreign and strange without her presence in my life. Even my time on the water yesterday was unsatisfying. Everything reminds me of her—at every I turn, I see her. I sit on my bed and bury my head in my arms. I'm at a total loss. I'm still angry from the way she acted while we were together, but a growing part of me worries if I let her go now I'll regret it for the rest of my life. I have a flashback of her eyes as she apologized, the clarity of the green-blue. Those mermaid eyes. I glance at my watch; it's now seven am.

She's leaving today.

I gallop out of the house before I know what's happening. All I know is I can't let her go this way. I jump into my Jeep, speeding straight for the inn and praying I don't miss her. I make it there in minutes and I'm running up the drive when her mother comes out the front door.

"She's not here, Tristan," she says. "She's at the airport—"

"What gate? No, wait, what airline? And when does she take off?"

"Jet Blue. She's supposed to leave in an hour."

I'm already running full speed for the Jeep again, even as Ms. LaVallie calls to me. All I can think is that I have to get there before she leaves. I can't let her go. I thought I could, but I can't. My pride would have let her leave, but my heart can't take it. She still has it in her hands.

I know the way to Logan airport, but even so it takes me too long. I sprint inside, searching wildly through the crowds. I have to catch her before she goes into the boarding area and I lose her. I barrel through the crowd, pushing people out of my way, but I don't see her anywhere. I spin around, searching for her face, but all I see are strangers. This is never going to work. This airport is huge, and if I can't get to her specific gate I'll miss her. I run my hands through my hair, panicking. I need to come up with a plan. If I can come up with some sort of plan it'll be all right.

"Tristan?"

I would know that voice anywhere. I spin around again, feeling a little dizzy, and there she is, standing with her suitcase. It's like an image from a dream. Her hair is falling in her face and she's looking at me quizzically, biting her lip.

"Emma," I say. "I'm sorry, for yesterday. I'm sorry—"

She drops her suitcase and runs into my arms, and her body against me is heaven all over again. She kisses me, her hands on my face, and I'm completely lost.

"It's okay," she says, gasping as I kiss her cheek, then her neck. "It's okay. I'm the one who should still be apologizing."

"No," I say. "I shouldn't have acted like I didn't care about you. Because I do, Emma."

"I know," she says, taking my face in her hands. She kisses me slow and soft, and my pulse races.

"I can't believe you came," she says finally, pulling back. "I thought I'd never see you again."

"Emma, don't go," I say, taking her hand. "Please, don't."

"Tristan, I'm coming back in a week."

I couldn't be more shocked if she'd smacked me upside the head. "What?"

"I talked it over with my parents and they both agreed. My dad thinks I'm ready for something new.

I'm going to work with my mom at the inn, and apply for college. If I get in I'll go next fall."

"When did all of this happen?"

"Yesterday." She covers her mouth with her hand as she starts laughing, and soon we are swaying back and forth, locked in each other's arms.

"I love you," I say into her neck. "I had to say it. I love you, and I'm sorry for everything."

She gives me a huge smile, like a sunbeam spreading across her face, and she's the most beautiful thing in the world.

"I love you," she whispers back, shyly, as though she's not used to saying it or hearing it. She'll get used to hearing it, though, if I have anything to say about it. "And I'm sorry, too."

"So, you're really coming back?"

"Yup. I just need a week to pack everything. But Tristan, they're calling me to board. I need to go." She steps toward me, cupping my cheek in her palm. Her beautiful eyes search mine.

"Will you be here when I get back?"

I kiss her again and again. "Yes. I'll be right here."

She kisses me, her lips branding me with something totally and uniquely Emma. She might have turned me completely inside out this summer, and she's frustrated me nearly as much as she's made me happy, but she's mine. I don't know how else to put it into words. She fills a part of me that I didn't realize was empty.

She walks to the boarding area with the biggest smile on her face that I've ever seen, waving goodbye. But she'll be back, I think to myself. And when she is I don't have to pretend anymore. I can just love her in the best way that I know how. Knowing she loves me has changed my entire perspective; this still might not be easy, but I'm more convinced than ever that we'll find a way to make it work perfectly for us. And somehow, in this moment, knowing that is enough.